CRAIG MARTELLE

MICHAEL ANDERLE

NOMAD'S FURY

A KUTHERIAN GAMBIT SERIES
TERRY HENRY WALTON CHRONICLES
BOOK 5

They say behind every great man, is a great woman,
but what if the woman is a Werewolf?

COPYRIGHT

DEDICATION

We can't write without those who support us
On the home front, we thank you for being there for us

We wouldn't be able to do this for a living if it weren't for our readers
We thank you for reading our books

Nomad's Fury
The Terry Henry Walton Chronicles
Team Includes

BETA / EDITOR BOOK
Acknowledgements in Back!

JIT Beta Readers - From both of us, our deepest gratitude!

Micky Cocker
Alex Wilson
Ginger Sparkman
Kimberly Boyer
Maria Stanley

*If I missed anyone, **please** let me know!*

PROLOGUE

Terry waved as the semi passed between the farms. He knew that Pepe and Maria would be all eyes when they saw the fertile fields. The people weren't as shy as they had been before. They weren't waving back, but they weren't running away either.

Terry wondered if Corporal James had been able to make contact. He'd find out soon enough.

The convoy limped off the exit and pulled into the parking area of the old power plant. The other vehicles pulled in behind, parking in order as they always did, side to side, so if a vehicle died in place, it wouldn't hold up the others.

Terry wondered if they were inside, curious that he couldn't hear anything. He realized that the main door was closed. When he got to it, there was a note scratched into the rust. "Home, 2 miles that way," with an arrow.

Terry jogged back to the others. All the vehicles were shut

down and people were staggering around, confused. Terry climbed into his dune buggy and stood on the driver's chair. He clung to the roll cage that made up the roof of the vehicle.

"Listen up," he projected, his voice echoing oddly off the old power plant. "This is the power plant that we will eventually bring online. But our people here left us a note. It says that our new home is two miles that way. I don't know about you, but after that drive, I could use the walk. HOME!"

The people cheered weakly. Terry hoped to hell that they were ready for the influx of people they were going to get.

"Need us to fire the trucks up, boss? One last time," Blevin asked.

"Let's see where we're going, First Sergeant, then we'll move things intelligently, one time, to the best place for them. It would be nice if you could get these into a shop, wouldn't it?"

The old man nodded, smiling.

"That it would, Colonel."

The clop of hooves on the roadway alerted the town's people.

James and Lacy waved from their horses. They negotiated the hill and rode through what used to be a gate and into the old power plant's parking lot.

They saw the colonel and made a beeline, stopping in front of him and saluting.

"Damn good to see you two!" Terry told them.

"You made some great time, sir. We weren't expecting you for quite a while," James started, looking around at the mass of people, many of them new.

"Report, Corporal," Terry ordered.

"Great Lakes Naval Base is right there," James reported, pointing. "It has a small power plant that Ted and Timmons have already been able to get running. We're currently cleaning out multi-family homes and barracks for the good people of New Boulder!"

James yelled the last part for everyone to hear.

"Is there room to park our trucks?"

"As much as you need, sir, and would you look at that! Where in the hell did you find all of this? Who are these people? Where's the rest of the platoon?" James asked rapidly, pointing to the equipment, then waving his arm at the mob of people.

Lacy shook her head and rolled her eyes, while a couple of the people they knew from New Boulder made their way close to shake her hand.

Billy and Felicity were happy to walk or drive the last mile. It didn't matter to them, they just wanted to get to their new home. Billy waited for Terry to give the order.

Char laughed and Terry smiled. "We'll talk later, Corporal, once we have these people settled. Blevin! Fire up the trucks. We're going home!"

Many opted to walk, while others climbed back into the vehicles. Three of the trucks wouldn't start. At that point, no one cared. People adjusted and the other engines revved.

Terry led the way in his dune buggy, driving easily down the cleared roadway. The other vehicles followed. James galloped ahead while Lacy remained with those walking.

James led them through the main gate and into the base, turning and following the road past sports fields, past the parade deck, and behind the main administration buildings where the temporary housing units were located.

James directed the vehicles into the largest parking lot. Terry waved Billy to the front. He drove up and parked his dune buggy next to Terry's beat up ride. James pointed as he told Billy about the available quarters that they'd already prepared. They only had half of what they needed, since they had thought they had more time.

Billy told them not to worry. They had four hundred people to help and what would have taken two people months to do, the town's people would accomplish in days.

Billy looked at the main building where admirals and naval captains would have once sat. "I see the mayor's office, Felicity darling."

"I do, too, Billy dear," Felicity drawled.

The sound of a train whistle pierced the late afternoon air.

"I should have told you that Timmons took the others to look for a steam engine so they could bring the Mini Cooper back here." James grinned.

"No way!" Terry jumped in the dune buggy where Char and Kae joined him.

"What's that noise, Mom?" Kaeden asked.

"That is a train, and I expect it is pulling humanity's future," Char replied.

CHAPTER ONE

Joseph stood on the road that ran between the two halves of the Great Lakes Naval Station.

The bustle of activity warmed his Vampire heart. So many hard-working, well-fed humans. The Werewolves bothered him, and the Were-tiger threw him for a loop.

"Where did you come from?" he asked himself. He tilted his head to keep the sun off his skin, the brim of his hat casting a wide shadow. The rest of his delicate skin was covered in black leather.

The group had arrived the previous day in vehicles. Vehicles! Maybe they weren't kidding when they said they were bringing civilization back. All that warm blood, pulses pounding, bodies writhing.

It gave him hope, which was something he hadn't had in a long, long time.

He watched and waited.

❖ ❖ ❖

"He's here," Char said, clenching her fists. "How about that, huh? Here less than a day and we get a Forsaken stopping by for a snack."

She walked out the front door of the guest quarters that James and Lacy had prepared for them, but the quality of their new home was forgotten in the presence of a Forsaken.

Char sensed the others and waited. Ted, Timmons, Sue, Shonna, and Merrit joined her. Terry and Kae stood nearby.

"Shall we?" Char asked, turning without waiting for a response.

"His name is Joseph," Timmons said softly, leaning backward to protect himself from an expected punch.

Char froze. "You've been talking with a Forsaken, and you didn't tell me before now?"

"I'm sorry, but you've been here for less than a day. There was so much, and this guy was scared off fairly easily. Look at him, he's just standing there, I suspect, waiting for us." Timmons wouldn't look Char in the eye.

She pursed her lips as she thought. "That may change things a bit, but if you and Ted intimidated him, then we'll talk first before killing him. Shall we?" Char walked casually with the rest of her pack, including the Were-tiger Aaron, noting that the Forsaken seemed to be waiting patiently.

She wondered if he thought of humans as snacks.

It disgusted her. Char's purple eyes sparkled and started to glow as the pack left the base and headed straight for the man in black. Terry and Kae walked right behind Char.

"I'm curious," Terry started to say as the group walked quickly along the road toward the waiting Vampire.

"Forsaken killed Xandrie," she replied, ice hanging from

her words. "The only thing I'm curious about is how quickly the blood can flow from his body after his head is cut off and on the ground."

Char strode boldly to Joseph, stopping when she was within arm's reach.

"Such hatred boiling behind that pretty face," Joseph said smoothly. Her lip twitched in revulsion at the pasty white of the unnatural skin on his face.

Terry grabbed her arm. She tried to shrug him off, but he gripped more tightly. Char turned on him, angry. He caressed her face and smiled. She relaxed and her eyes sparkled back at him. She took Kaeden's hand.

At dizzying speed, Terry rotated at his waist and swung, catching the Forsaken in the middle of the chest with the heel of his hand. Like a battering ram, it drove the Vampire backward and threw him off his feet.

With a grunt, Joseph hit the ground and lay there.

"Get up," Terry demanded, a snarl on his face as he loomed over the Vampire.

Joseph let himself start healing from the cracked sternum the human had just given him, something the Forsaken considered to be impossible. He'd seen in Terry's mind that he was going to hit him, but had no idea the power that would be behind it.

"I just came to talk. I could have snatched one of your people in the night and you would have never known, but I didn't. Here I am, hat in hand, and you go all Thor the Avenger on me," Joseph grumbled as he struggled to his feet. "It's been a while, but okay. Give me a second."

"The only thing I'll give you is more of you on the ground, crying like a little girl," Terry said as he stalked to the side. The Werewolves were spreading out, forming a large circle from which the Vamp couldn't escape.

"Well now, that's a bit unfair, don't you think?" Joseph asked as he regained his feet and started stretching.

"Marine Corps rules, suckwad. The only fair fight is the one you lose," Terry quoted.

Joseph mumbled something, then started stretching, but not as a fighter preparing to fight, more like a ballerina preparing for a performance. He dipped, holding one hand over his head, shifting left and then right, hopping from his heel to his toes.

Char looked confused. Terry wondered what the creature's game was.

The Forsaken hopped forward one step while holding a pose, then spun, sending a roundhouse toward Terry's head.

The human caught Joseph's foot and dropped, bunching his legs underneath him as he twisted and pulled, lifting the Forsaken. Terry swung him through one hundred and eighty degrees and slammed him into the ground.

"Oh, that hurt," Joseph grunted, as he lay with pavement embedded in his face. He crawled to his knees and Terry kicked him in the ribs, sending the Forsaken halfway across their circle. Shonna stepped back. Joseph looked up at her through foggy eyes. She responded by drawing a line across her throat with one finger.

He looked afraid, but summoned the courage to stand and face his attacker.

"Do you know how long I've been alive?" Joseph asked, looking at the faces before him, the Were with the human child hiding behind her, the other Werewolves, and finally the human with the slight red glow to his eyes.

"I don't care," Terry said as he slowly approached.

"Four hundred, forty-seven years. I came over on one of

the original settlement ships. Unlimited land to do with as we wished, to make our own way, be beholden to no one. I've seen how this country grew, and how it ended. What if I told you that I don't drain people?" Joseph offered.

"Then I would call you a liar," Terry said.

Timmons interjected, "Then who drained that poor sap on the railroad line north of O'Hare?"

Terry snarled. "I'm pretty sure there's nothing you can say that will spare your life. You see, I wasn't here at the beginning, but I was here for the end, and fuckers like you? You didn't make any of it better. So we're cleaning house, starting fresh. Why would we want to include something as old and worn out as you?"

"At one point in my life, I lived in Williamsburg with the others, Thomas Jefferson, James Monroe, Patrick Henry, the Marquis de Lafayette. Do you know who Alexander Purdie was?" Joseph tilted his head to make sure he caught the look in Terry's eye. "I see you do. I was his partner in the printing business. John Joseph Dixon. I simply go by Joseph now."

Terry hesitated. Purdie had printed the materials used to build support for the revolution.

"But you were bought out of the business in seventeen seventy-five?" Terry asked, stepping back to give them space. He'd read all he could on the revolution, including taking numerous trips to Colonial Williamsburg. He was a big fan of history.

"I sold him my share of the business, but I was still there through it all. Even joined the army at one point, early in seventy-six. They needed people with all different skills. Washington was magnificent, by the way. His memoirs and storytellers don't do him justice," Joseph continued as he circled staying out of Terry's reach.

Char lunged in and shoved the Vampire forward. He stumbled a couple steps. Terry hit him in the face with a right jab, driving the Forsaken to the ground.

He moaned as he lay there, unwilling to move and expose himself to the slow torture of a ritual pummeling.

Joseph had been in Terry's mind, saw the man's honor code, and most importantly for the Forsaken, saw a way to survive the day.

"I will work for you," Joseph told Terry, from one knee, while clasping his hands behind his head. "You have my word that I will take no lives from your group."

Terry wanted to punch him, but he couldn't attack someone who surrendered. Char could because of her abject hatred for the Forsaken.

"Hold!" Terry growled as he moved to Joseph's side.

"What would that look like, Joseph?" Terry asked, crouching to be closer to a Vampire, who looked to be in a great deal of pain. His hat had come off and was under Merrit's foot as the Werewolf stood there, arms crossed, glaring. "A Forsaken working for a lowly human…"

"I know not what you are or even what your name is, but 'lowly human' is not it. I've never seen the red glow from anyone other than one of my kind. You, good sir, are something different and something special. If civilization is to return, it will be because you carry it on your *back*." Joseph squinted as he looked up at Terry, who had put the sun behind him as a little extra torment for the daywalker.

"My name is Terry Henry Walton, Colonel, Force de Guerre. This is Major Charumati, my partner, and our son Kaeden. If I let you live," Terry started to say, but the Werewolves growled, stamped their feet, and clenched their fists in dismay. They wanted nothing more than to see the

Forsaken die. "If I let you live, how can you assure me of your loyalty?"

"Nice to meet you, Terry Henry Walton, Charumati, Kaeden. I'm afraid that all I have are my actions, from which you can judge me. I have not attacked any of your people and will not from this day forward, but to be sure, I need to know who your people are and where they will be," Joseph said with his head up, looking at Terry. He kept his hands clenched behind his head.

Char's lip curled as she snarled and glared at the creature.

"See, Joseph, that's the rub. We're not going to roll our people out to be your personal smorgasbord. Many of them were trapped underground for the past two decades with some Forsaken. Their necks are scarred from the feedings over the years. I find that thought repulsive and your very existence to be a blight on humanity." Terry took a breath before continuing. His eyes glowed as he leaned close.

"Here's the deal. If we let you go, and at some point in time, you bite one of our people, I will hunt you down and cut your limbs off, one by one. Then I will drag your half-living carcass around as I kill anything and anyone you ever cared about. I will burn down city blocks just to make sure. You will suffer greatly before you die. Look into my mind, Joseph. Can you see it?"

Terry thought about Melissa's murder and his vengeance. He fingered the silvered blade hidden in his shirt, a remnant from that time.

"It's not very pretty," Joseph replied, finally standing but keeping his hands where they were. "I agree to your terms. I will not betray you or them."

Joseph finally lowered his arms, carefully, and he swept one around the circle to take in everyone present.

Char snarled, the anger growing within her. Terry held his hands out to calm her and mouthed the words, "Trust me."

She closed her eyes and breathed deeply. Kaeden stood at her side, holding her hand and watching Terry.

The boy wasn't afraid.

"Where are you staying?" Terry asked. Joseph shrugged. "There we go, trust issues. I asked you a question and need an answer. We will tell our people to avoid that area, but if you aren't going to tell us, then we're back to square one."

Terry pulled his silvered blade and twirled it in the sunshine. "I live in the city, in the basement of the tallest building," Joseph offered, looking at the ground. Terry pointed to the hat and motioned for Merrit to give it to him. The Werewolf snarled and kept his foot on it.

Terry walked up to the man, getting inches from his face. "I don't know you that well, Merrit, but I'm your alpha and I've given you an order. If you don't want to end up bloody and broken, I suggest you give me that fucking hat," Terry growled.

Merrit looked quickly away. He'd learned the previous night that Char had removed Timmons's hand. The new alphas would not tolerate disobedience or even disrespect. Merrit had just watched Terry Henry Walton beat the snot out of a Vampire without breaking a sweat. Even though the Vamp was a weaker daywalker, he was still a Forsaken, just like the one that had ended Xandrie's life.

Merrit knew that Terry was not to be toyed with. He mumbled an apology, then picked up the leather hat, dusted it off, and handed it to Terry.

"Thank you," he replied, snatching it from Merrit's fingers and glaring at him for an instant before turning to the Forsaken. "Here."

MARTELLE AND ANDERLE

Joseph put the hat on his head, angling it slightly to best block the sun. "I will return in three days' time to meet with you, Terry Henry Walton, and every three days thereafter, to demonstrate my good faith and see if there is anything you require of me."

Terry thrust his hand out. Joseph looked at it. He didn't remove his glove as he took the human's hand, gripped it firmly, and shook twice before leaving go. Joseph bowed deeply to Char, then walked through the gap between Timmons and Shonna without looking at either of them. He walked away, limping slightly while holding his side.

They turned to watch him go.

"He's my responsibility and none of you need doubt that I will do what I said I would if he betrays us. If that's all there is to this happy meet and greet, we have shit to do and we're burning daylight." Terry scowled as he looked at the bunch.

No one seemed happy, except Aaron, and he was happy all the time, regardless of what was going on.

"Back to the base, all of you," Char said in a low voice, not taking her eyes from TH. "We'll be along shortly. I'd like to talk with my husband alone."

CHAPTER TWO

"Everett, Hayden, tell me something of yourselves," Adams asked as they sat around the campfire, somewhere along the Missouri River. The herd grazed at the water's edge, shuffling slowly about. The cows from both herds intermingled as if they'd always been together, and they were equally tired, too.

The children of Eli looked at each other and then at Adams. They rarely spoke, and when they did, it was softly.

"What's there to tell? We were born before the fall, lived decent lives and then we were refugees within our own world. Thank God—" The two crossed themselves. "—for our father who already lived a minimalist existence, off the grid, as they would say, before there was no more grid."

Everett talked slowly, spoke deliberately.

"What did you do for fun?" Adams pressed.

"We would challenge each other in getting the chores

done. After services on Sunday, we'd play rock toss!" Everett's excitement increased and Hayden nodded and smiled.

Adams was from New York City. He had a vastly different idea of what it was like to have fun. Chuck the rock would not have been in his top one thousand things to do when trying to have fun. But this was a new world.

"Is it light enough? Show me what you mean and let's play," Adams suggested. EssCee and Lousy State leaned in. Alabama decided he wanted to play, too. Clemson and Vandy were at the far side of the small pasture, keeping the cattle from wandering off. They didn't know there was a game afoot.

Those driving the carts had made a separate camp a little ways away, cordoning the cattle so no one had to play shepherd during the night. The cattle remained contained. Each morning when they rose, numerous people would count the heads to make sure none strayed during the night. Only twice did any of the Force de Guerre have to hunt down strays and drive them back to the herd.

Hayden jumped up first, but then stopped and waited, since she had been raised to defer to her brothers. Adams didn't give a rat's ass. "Hayden, tell us the rules," Adams said.

She looked to Everett, who nodded slightly.

Adams wanted to punch them both. The five youngsters, only one of whom was Hayden's, stood in a line behind their relatives. They wouldn't ask to play, but were eager and ready if invited.

"You, too! Everyone plays. If Terry Henry Walton has taught us anything, it's that everyone gets an equal chance to participate. Equal opportunity, but not equal result. You are what you make of yourselves, right?" Adams hadn't heard Terry say any of that stuff, but Char told them how it was going to be. He assumed she got it from her mate because that wasn't anything like what she'd said before meeting the human.

"You take one big rock and two small rocks. Mark the small ones so you know which ones are yours. First person throws their big rock. Then everyone else throws one of their small rocks. If someone hits the big rock, that round is over. Everyone goes to that spot and whoever hit it throws their big rock. You keep track of how many times you get to throw your big rock. If no one hits the target rock, then we throw the second small stone. If no one hits it again, then closest throws the next target rock. That's it," she narrated in an excited little girl voice.

They found their rocks and did their best to mark them. Everett threw the target rock to start things off. Lousy State went first. He wound up like a major league pitcher and lined a fastball straight into the target rock that was only twenty feet away. He hit it, much to everyone else's dismay.

They trooped to that spot, where Lousy launched his target rock a good hundred feet into the distance.

"We don't usually throw them that far," Hayden whispered as the group pressed in on her, angling to get their turn to throw at the target.

"Looks like we have a higher level of competition," Adams replied, making sure the youngest went first. They accurately threw their rocks, but no one hit the target. Everett and Hayden were the two farthest away, so they would go first in the next round. Alabama had made the closest toss. He recovered his two small stones and got ready to heave his target rock as if he wanted to outdo his brother.

"Not as far, big dog," Adams cautioned. The young man groaned, but threw the big rock a little closer.

Eli's grandchildren huddled around Everett and Hayden.

MARTELLE AND ANDERLE

Everett leaned close to Adams. "I'm not sure we should be playing our game with the darkies," he whispered.

Adams grabbed the man by the throat. "What the fuck just came out of your mouth?" Everett struggled to breathe. Hayden and the five children dropped to their knees and bowed their heads. "You look at them through the lens of their skin? I just lost my mate to a white-skinned demon. Do I clump you fuckers in with him? No. If I ever hear or see you do anything that suggests they are second-class citizens because they are different from you, I will beat you senseless and leave you for dead! You fuckers are the different ones, if you ask me. Now get the hell up there and play, it's your turn, and the rest of us are waiting!"

The Weathers boys were taken aback. They'd never been exposed to anything like that before. The WWDE was the great equalizer, making most people equally dead, regardless of skin color or social status. Adams thought Werwolves were higher up the food chain than the humans, but he kept that to himself. He was in charge of getting the cattle and these people to New Chicago and by all that was holy, he was going to make it happen.

"Game's on and I'm going to get serious and kick all your lame asses!" Adams challenged. The slight was quickly forgotten as Adams mixed the players up, then created a team challenge, forming teams with various players on each side.

After it got too dark to continue, Adams sent everyone to their blankets to rest. Tomorrow was going to be a long day, even though he had nothing special planned, tomorrows were always long days.

"Wait up, you two," he told Everett and Hayden. "Please, it's just us out here. We need each other, respect each other. We have a long ways to go, and I don't have time to deal with hurt feelings or other bullshit, so please, everyone here is equal."

Everett tried to apologize, but Adams stopped him. "That's the end of it. We'll play the game every night from now until we get to our new home, because it's fun! I would have never thought about it, but it's fun. We may even have to start a league because we have so many players."

"What's a league?" Everett asked.

"And that is for another day. Thanks for sharing your game with the rest of us. That made a good difference tonight. Listen. You can still hear them laughing." Adams smiled and clapped Everett on the back. He hugged Hayden, probably longer than she was comfortable with, but he didn't want anyone living in a shell. He was from New York City, and that was just how it had to be.

He turned to walk away, but there was a commotion near the carts. He took off running.

❖ ❖ ❖

Terry was prepared for the fight of the century. He could see that Char wasn't happy. In fact, he thought that she was furious, but that word probably didn't cover how angry she was.

"You let a Forsaken go," she said in a low and dangerous voice.

"Yes, I did," he replied simply. She got close and swung with the considerable power in her body. Terry closed his eyes without raising his arms or defending himself. Char pulled her punch at the last instant, just clipping the tip of Terry's nose and that was enough to flatten it against his face.

He grunted, but didn't move. Kaeden started to cry. She picked the boy up and stood there.

When Terry opened his eyes, he saw the tears running from Char's beautiful purple eyes. He didn't know what to say, but he knew what to do. He hugged his wife as best he could with Kae hugging her neck.

"I know why you did what you did, TH, and I also know that you're right. All I can say is these pregnancy hormones are a royal bitch," she whispered, quickly collecting herself and smiling at Kaeden. "And he's a Forsaken. Is there really room for them in a new world?"

She put the boy down and they each took a hand as they started walking back to the base. Not far off, Timmons was waiting.

"Would you look at that?" Char said when she saw that Timmons's hand had grown back. She was surprised that she hadn't noticed before then.

"I take nothing for granted, my alpha," he replied humbly. She slapped him on the shoulder. "The process was quite painful, for reference, but Kiwi and Gerry saved our lives, Ted's and mine both."

"I love hearing good things that my people have done, just like the good work you and Ted did in the decision to move here and use the better plant. That was top notch, Timmons," Terry replied.

"I had forgotten one other little tidbit that I figured you'd want to know…" Timmons stalled before saying the second part. Char's eyes were still puffy and Terry's nose was still flattened across his face. Timmons kept staring until Terry snapped it back into place, giving the nanocytes less to do. Kae giggled.

"There's a Were-bear in the area. Ted and I sensed it up near Milwaukee, where we were fishing from the sailboat, but we hauled ass out of there before he got too close. We don't think he followed us as that was, hell, a couple weeks ago and we haven't sensed anything since." Timmons looked out from under shaded eyes.

"You have a boat?" Terry asked. He used to love sailing.

"A Were-bear?" she asked, looking at Terry Henry.

"Please don't punch me in the face!" Timmons blurted.

Char turned back to her fellow Werewolf. "Why would you think I was going to punch you in the face?" She leaned closer to him and he started to raise a hand to protect himself, but fought the urge and forced it back to his side. He leaned away, turning slightly in case he needed to run.

Terry chuckled. "Until that baby is born, I think we're all going to be running for our lives," Terry quipped. Char turned back, leading with the stink-eye, and Timmons bolted.

Terry started to laugh, while massaging his nose, which Kaeden found funny and laughed along.

Char couldn't be angry with that. "You're heading the right way for a smacked bottom, mister," she told Terry, nudging him as he used Kaeden as a shield to hold her off.

"What should we worry about with a Were-bear?" Terry finally asked, his smile gone.

"No idea, honey. No idea at all, but the pack is back together, mostly. We're better able to handle a Were-bear now if need be, although I suspect one would simply avoid the area. Too much Were blood here for him or her to enter our territory." Char shrugged and started walking back to the base.

"Let's hope that the bear steers clear, while planning what we need to do if it shows up. You know me—hope for the best, prepare for the worst," Terry said as he looked behind him at the road where Joseph had been.

"Maybe we can talk the Were-bear into joining us? He

might be able to teach Hank some manners," Terry suggested, cocking one eyebrow.

"This isn't a town, it's a zoo!" Char declared.

Kaeden whispered into Terry's ear. "What's a zoo?"

Terry kept his mouth shut. It didn't help that Clyde was barking somewhere nearby.

"I miss my dog," he said to no one in particular.

❖ ❖ ❖

Mark wanted a barracks for the Force personnel to call their own. On the side of the base intended for recruit training, there were numerous barracks of the type preferred by the military, but open squad bays, as Terry called them, didn't work for long-term residents. He was strongly opposed to such an arrangement, although Mark was in favor, selfishly, as his way of controlling the people.

The sergeant coordinated with Corporal James to determine that there were no other spaces that compared. Mark decided that they would modify the barracks to separate out the living spaces, creating small rooms for each person. The barracks building was three stories high with one wing on each side of a central stairway.

James suggested that it would only be temporary as scattered throughout the base, there was probably room for ten thousand people in a variety of homes and residential buildings.

The spaces in the recruit barracks were trashed with metal bunks thrown about haphazardly. Most of the mattresses were gone. Some of the windows had been broken out. There was a single enclosed room in each squad bay which the instructors used to use as an office. Mark directed Blackie to prepare that room, so it would look warm and friendly.

To Mark, the place was heaven. But when it came down to it, it wasn't home. They needed something that they were missing. Mark ordered the platoon to continue working while he went in search of the missing piece.

An hour later, he found Mrs. Grimes.

"We'd like you to come live with us," Mark asked, his hat in his hand and wearing his uniform, including his flak jacket as they always did.

"Why would I want to do that?" she asked, fishing for a compliment.

"Because we need you to keep us in line. We have a barracks, but we don't have a plan. You saved us from having to worry about that stuff back in New Boulder. We need you to do that here. We have a completely separate room that is just for you," he teased. "What do you say, Mrs. Grimes?"

"Let me see it first, before I make any decisions," she replied.

"You miss us, don't you?" he taunted the old woman. She produced her spoon at the speed of light and rapped it across his knuckles. He winced and muttered, "I don't miss that, that's for sure!"

She'd already decided that they needed her if they were going to be decent human beings.

She had a plan.

CHAPTER THREE

When Adams reached the carts, he found the people sitting around a small fire, relaxing after their evening meal.

"What the hell happened?"

"Cow got caught in the harness. She got out of it pretty quickly. No harm no foul, right?" the old farmer said.

Adams shook his head, before going on a mini-walkabout. He liked to walk in the darkness around the separate camps each night so he could get fresh air and clear his head. It gave him time alone to think about Xandrie and about what a way ahead looked like.

He was lonely and found that being alone helped. He moved farther into the darkness, where he carefully undressed and turned into his Were self. He ran free, hunting and acting like a pup. He wanted to recover the innocence of youth when he had nothing to worry about.

Adams knew it would never be the same, but Char had told them how Terry had lost his whole family, yet there he was, giving one hundred percent of himself so that others could live in peace. Life would never be the same, but if it was worse, that was Adams's fault. For it to be better, that was Adams's responsibility.

He had committed to the alpha that he would get the cattle to New Chicago. Adams also knew that his mission was to bring the people too, as one group and not a bunch of individuals. Tonight had moved them one step closer to that goal.

He couldn't control how people felt, but he could influence how they perceived the world around them. Eli's family wasn't all bad, once he got to know them. Same with all the kids, the farmers, everyone.

Adams ran down a jackrabbit, devoured it, and then chased away a couple coyotes. He returned to his clothes, changed, and tried to fall asleep. It never came easy and when it did, it wasn't restful. Forsaken leapt at him from the darkness, and Xandrie's screams echoed through his mind.

❖ ❖ ❖

"Ted, you sly dog!" Terry said, as he decided that he had to mess with Ted, the master of the literal word.

"I'm a Werewolf," he said, confused.

"But you have a boat, my man!" Terry slapped Ted on the back.

"Yes!" Ted brightened appreciably. "It holds three people and has been stalwart under the general conditions of the lake. We've only sailed within sight of land, I'm afraid. I dare not take it farther out. It's too small for that."

"When do we go?" Terry pressed.

"We have a rather lengthy list of things to do here," Ted replied and then he started going through it. Terry stopped him while Char watched.

"No problem, Ted. Do you mind if I take your boat out? I was ASA certified in small boat and coastal navigation. That was a while ago, but it won't take long to get back up to speed. Looks like light winds today," Terry noted. He grinned at Ted, knowing the man would cave at the mention of certifications.

"I guess, but it's my boat!" Ted countered.

"We'll return it better than it was when we left," Terry called over his shoulder as he waved and walked away. Char and Kae followed him out of the small power plant.

"I doubt that. It's in perfect condition right now," Ted said to their fleeing forms.

Char huffed as Terry rushed ahead. He quickly realized the error of his ways, stopping and waiting for his family. Kae ran to him.

"What is sailing?" the boy asked.

"That, my little man, is what we are going to start teaching you. We'll use the wind to power us over the water. Look out there!" Terry pointed at the lake, its blue waters disappearing over the distance. It was an ocean as far as Kaeden was concerned. He hugged Terry tightly, afraid of the vast unknown.

"We'll stay close to the shore as we head north, maybe do some fishing, check out the area, see if we sense a Were-bear, you know, the usual stuff," Terry said.

Char shook her head, knowing that she didn't want to tangle with any such thing.

"I left my fishing spear!" Kae cried, wiggling to get down.

"We don't need that for this kind of fishing. We'll use

lines and lures. I'll show you and we'll have fun." Terry put Kae down, and the boy ran ahead.

"Were-bear? What is wrong with you?" Char's look made him stop. He held his hands up, wondering what she was talking about.

"See the great Terry Henry Walton wrestling a man eater in the center ring!" Char continued in her best rendition of a circus ringmaster.

"I guess that's what it looks like, but that's not what it is," Terry started as he took Char's hand and they walked slowly along the shore on their way to the small harbor where Ted's boat was docked. "I want to keep any potential enemies away from here. Peace starts out there, not in here."

"You'll fight him, won't you?" Char asked.

"I would prefer not to, actually. I doubt this old .45 would do anything besides piss him off. The rifle? That, too. Maybe a grenade?" Terry smiled. "I'm kidding. I have no intention of going ashore to engage with a Were-bear. I just want to know where it is."

Char understood where he was coming from. If they had to stare down such a creature, she wanted to do it with the pack on one side of her and Terry and the platoon on the other.

❖ ❖ ❖

Mrs. Grimes was in a state. After all of Mark's sweet-talking, when she showed up at the barracks, she found the entire platoon playing grab-ass and nothing was clean. She refused to take more than one step into the squad bay. The sergeant was none too pleased either.

He invited her outside to wait where there was a picnic

table. He used his sleeve to clear off a spot and then stormed back inside. Mrs. Grimes was gratified to hear the yelling and commotion as large pieces of furniture were thrown about.

More yelling. She kicked back and closed her eyes to absorb the sun without feeling like she was roasting alive.

❖ ❖ ❖

Aaron stood on the outside looking in. He hadn't been accepted by the pack, although he'd made overtures. Shonna and Merrit had joined two other Werewolves in the power plant. That left Sue, and she was busy with the mayor as he tried to figure out how to feed the people.

The native delegation was every bit as displaced as he was. That was where he'd been found, but hadn't fit in. He asked the chief if he could join the delegation, although the chief told him that he didn't need to ask. He was a free man to do as he wished. Since they'd taken him in, he decided he'd help Chief Foxtail's mother. At least until someone else accepted him for who he was.

The old lady moved slowly and wanted it warmer. "Autumn Dawn, we will build a fire for you," the man called Rapids said soothingly. The old woman was uncomfortable and they hoped that her age wasn't getting the best of her.

"Winter Rain, I need you to gather more firewood," Rapids requested of the last in their party, the young man at the age to prove himself.

"I'll go with him," Aaron offered and Rapids nodded.

"Winter Rain, where do you think we can find some firewood?" Aaron asked congenially.

The young man looked hard at the tall man. He seemed

to study Aaron for a few moments before shrugging and walking away.

Aaron looked at the ground as he shuffled after the young man. *I just wanted to teach English, but then this, I'm a Were,* he thought.

Next door to the base was an old golf course. Nature had reclaimed the land and that meant deadfall, logs scattered on the ground that could be hacked up and used for a fire.

The snarl of the wolf pack was the first sound they heard. Both men froze, refusing to move. Ten wolves moved in around them, many baring their fangs and growling. Aaron started to back up. They moved toward him, ignoring Winter Rain.

The first wolf darted in, angling for the leg of its enemy, hobble it so the others could close in for the kill.

Aaron wasn't going to let that happen. He instantly changed into a Were-tiger, shaking off the human clothes as he slapped the attacking wolf aside. With one mighty leap, he hit the side of the tree, digging in his claws, and he ran upwards to the first broad branch.

The wolves threw themselves at the base of the tree, looking up, growling and snapping.

The Were-tiger let out an ear-piercing scream. Winter Rain covered his ears and gasped. The wolf pack backed away, but still surrounded the tree. They looked as if they wished the branch would break. Aaron screamed again, his pale-yellow eyes blazing with rage.

He picked his target, flexed his paws, felt the claws respond against the tree bark, and prepared to leap.

❖ ❖ ❖

Boris had to ride down two of the longhorns who wandered off. Once he chased them back, the group drove the herd ahead, keeping the Missouri River to their left.

Adams watched from the seat of the cart. Fred was driving as he usually did, casually without saying a word.

"I've ridden with you, what, five times now?" Adams asked. The man nodded and mumbled. "I think you have yet to say a word. What's up, Fred? Why didn't you stay behind like Ernie?"

The older man looked at Adams as if he was too young to know any better. "Even an idiot could see that Boulder was dying. I give it five years and the Wastelands will be crawling into the mountains. Boulder, Denver, all of it will be buried in red dust. You aren't old enough to know what it was like before," Fred replied.

Adams didn't correct the man regarding his age, but Fred was right in that Adams didn't know what Boulder was like before. He was a big city boy, born and raised.

"Green everywhere you looked. To the east? Massive fields and pastures. I lived out that way, had me a big farm, needed semis to haul my crops. Then that bullshit from the guvmint ruined me, ruined the whole world," Fred said bitterly.

"They ruined it for everyone, especially themselves," Adams responded slowly. "No one from the government survived, I suspect—they were hit with the worst of it. Governments fighting governments and us poor saps caught in the middle." Adam thought about it a moment, "It made the Greek tragedies look like comedies."

They rode on in silence as the cattle ambled onward.

Adams called a halt when he saw a group of Native Americans blocking the way ahead.

He shouted at those ahead of him to pass the word and after five minutes, the Weathers boys and Eli's grandkids had the herd stopped.

Adams jumped from the buckboard and walked quickly around the small herd, studiously avoiding the massive horns of Eli's cattle that seemed to find their way into his path.

❖ ❖ ❖

The small boat slid gracefully through the water as Terry tacked back and forth, calling out the warning each time so Char and Kae wouldn't get clocked by the boom as it snapped from port to starboard and back again.

Kaeden stood in the boat, leaning over the front so he could see straight ahead. Terry was keeping it one hundred yards offshore where the lake was still relatively shallow, but free of underwater obstructions.

"Can you swim?" he asked Char.

"Of course," she answered dismissively, then winked at him. "But I only dog paddle."

He appreciated the humor. "What about you, Kae? Can you swim?" The boy turned and instantly looked sad. He shook his head and stared into the bottom of the boat.

"What's that face for?" Terry chuckled. "The world is your classroom and it's our responsibility to teach you. We'll make sure you learn how to swim. Climb back here and help me steer."

Char looked at the serenity of the water as Kae grabbed the tiller and held on. "Shouldn't we be helping with the million things that need to be done?" Char asked.

"Yes, we should, but in due time. Our job is to keep these people safe so they can do what they do, survive, thrive, all of that," Terry said as he watched the wind and the waves. He tacked the boat toward shore, then continued.

"They need to settle in. If we were there, they'd ask us questions that are best asked of Billy Spires and the town elders. I think the most important thing we can do is find out if we have a Were-bear problem. If he or she is up here, then we'll get the pack and come back, armed to the teeth. We don't need that kind of problem; just like we don't need to worry about a Forsaken. Keep your friends close and your enemies closer, right?"

Char pursed her lips as she thought about it. After an hour of sailing, Kae was getting tired, so they settled into a sheltered cove and dropped a couple lines in the water. Char was rewarded with the first catch, while Terry helped Kae to bring in the second fish. After that, they quickly filled the bottom of the boat.

Char continued fishing while Terry taught Kaeden how to clean the mass of walleyes that they'd landed. The boy used his own knife to gut some of them, but didn't have the strength to cut off the head. In due time, strength and a sharp blade would serve the boy well.

During the fight within Cheyenne Mountain, Terry's knife was duller than it should have been and it cost him time. In a fight with a Forsaken, the last thing there was to waste was time. He'd never sheathed a dull blade after that, meticulously caring for his one tool that had been effective against all his enemies. His trusty bullwhip was a close second.

"Oh, no," Char said, eyes unfocused as she reached out with her senses. Terry knew the look only too well.

"How far?" Terry asked.

"A ways, but he's still here," Char replied.

"I guess we had best get back, then. We have a bear hunt to prepare for."

CHAPTER FOUR

What you're telling me is that you took a plant that was shielded from the EMP and meticulously shut down and it still took you a couple months to bring it online?" Shonna needled Timmons.

"How about you go fuck yourself!" Timmons replied angrily. The others laughed. "Yeah, very funny. We have some fifteen thousand gallons of fuel oil on hand. It'd be nice if we had a few tanker loads, but we need power to fill the pipeline and then pump it in here. That's just until we get the Mini Cooper online."

Ted wanted to show off his baby, and they wanted to see it. They had left the plant and stopped by the main building to pick up Sue when they heard the Were-tiger's scream.

Ted listened for an instant before running at Werewolf speed toward the sound. "I'm coming!" he yelled.

The others bolted after him. They charged through a section of downed fence and straight toward where they sensed the Were-tiger.

Ted bellowed unintelligibly. The others caught up to him as a Were-tiger launched itself from a branch into the wolf pack. Ted dove and intercepted the creature mid-leap. They tangled and rolled across the ground. The other Werewolves ran into the mix and pulled the Were-tiger off Ted, who suffered from a bite on his shoulder and scratches down his back.

He groaned as the others held the tiger's legs and punched it mercilessly. It struggled and screamed, unable to dig its fangs into anyone. The Were-tiger changed back into human form. Timmons punched the man in the side of his head, knocking him out.

The wolf pack growled as Ted struggled to his feet.

❖ ❖ ❖

Terry was quiet as he trimmed the sail to get the most speed from the port-side wind. Progress was slower on the southern leg than it had been going north. Char was reclining, her shirt pulled up to expose her body to the sun. Kae and Terry had their shirts off as they both hung on to the tiller.

"Relax," Char said. Her eyes were closed, but she knew her husband was anxious.

"It's hard," he admitted, checking the wind and trimming the sail two more clicks.

"Now you know. We'll set something up when we get back, and then we'll go say hi to our neighbor. Until then, enjoy the sun, the sea, and your sunbathing wife." Char smiled. Terry imagined her wearing sunglasses and a small bikini.

"Is that a baby bump?" Terry asked, looking closely.

"Yes, four months left to D-Day," she replied.

"Four! It should be eight," Terry argued.

"Don't refer to our offspring as it, please. Werewolves have a shorter gestation period. You might not want to blink, you may miss it." Terry sat there slack-jawed.

"Men…" Char lamented.

"Well, roll me in butter and fry me as a fritter!" Terry exclaimed.

Char opened her eyes and studied her grinning husband. "Where the hell did that linguistic assault on the senses come from?"

"Sorry, I was spending time with some of the survivors from the mountain. There were a few who referred to themselves as good ol' boys." Terry smiled, showing his perfect teeth.

"Don't ever say that again. Ever," she suggested, shutting her eyes and arching her back against the boat. Terry forgot about everything besides what was right in front of him.

"Yes, dear," he whispered, enjoying her beauty.

❖ ❖ ❖

The Werewolf pack carried Aaron's unconscious form back to the base and deposited him on the floor of Billy's office. The wolf pack waited outside while the humans went into the building. The population of New Boulder was not used to having a wolf pack in their midst so there was tension in the air.

The pack wasn't too keen on the idea of so many humans, either, but Ted kept them calm. It helped that the humans shied away from the pack as it loped from here to there.

MARTELLE AND ANDERLE

Aaron stirred and Shonna threw his clothes at him.

He looked around before reaching up to feel the bruises on his face. "I fear that I've made a mess of things, haven't I?" It wasn't a question. The scowls on the faces of the others told him everything he needed to know.

"I'll get my things and go," he said, shrugging into his clothes.

"You'll do no such thing," croaked an old woman's voice. They turned as Autumn Dawn shuffled in, helped by the young man who'd been with Aaron. "If your wolves hadn't attacked this young man, he would not have had to defend himself."

Aaron remembered the wolf pack closing in and nothing else. He couldn't be a witness at his own trial.

"Is that true?" Billy Spires asked.

The group looked to Ted for an answer. He shifted uncomfortably in his torn clothing. The healing process was underway, but Ted was still in pain. "Yes, but they saw him as a mountain cat. Everyone knows that wolves and cats don't get along."

"That settles it. Where in the hell did that wolf pack come from anyway?" Billy asked. Since they drove from New Boulder, Billy had no time to sit with Terry Henry and learn the details of his trip.

"We ran across them not far from New Boulder. Ted schooled them because I only had one hand at the time. He's their alpha," Timmons explained, pointing to Ted with some pride.

Billy studied Timmons's arms, confused at seeing two hands.

"I got better," Timmons said matter-of-factly, putting his hands in his pockets to take the attention away.

"We'll keep them separate," Ted suggested, looking hopefully at Billy, sniffing the air to smell his friends, both Were and wolf alike.

"No. That won't do," Billy said, putting his foot down. "You train them to accept him. Period."

Ted's lip curled involuntarily, and expressions darkened.

Billy answered Ted's body language. "I'll talk with Terry Henry and Char when they get back. We'll see if they're willing to kick out one of the native delegation."

"He's not one of them!" Shonna said, pointing at the tall man.

"He most assuredly is," the old woman said boldly.

No one argued with her. Felicity moved from a spot behind Billy and helped the old woman to a seat. Ever since meeting with the natives, she'd been avoiding them, but couldn't any longer.

Kill them with kindness. It had been successful in dealing with Charumati, and the base was too small to have enemies. Felicity resigned herself to her role as peacemaker.

Autumn Dawn looked into Felicity's eyes long and hard before accepting her help. When she did, she patted the young woman's arm affectionately. "Don't you mind Foxtail, dear. He's kind of old-fashioned," Dawn whispered.

Felicity had no idea what she was talking about, but she accepted the smile as genuine, just like her relief at not being on the receiving end of the old woman's ire.

"Aaron, how are you?" she asked as she sat in the rough overstuffed chair that looked out of place compared to the big metal desk behind which Billy sat in a rough metal chair.

Furious barking signaled Clyde and Sue's arrival. Ted ran outside and after a brief amount of yelling and scuffling, Sue walked in carrying a bleeding Clyde who had his tail tucked between his legs. Ted followed her and gave Billy both thumbs up.

"What kind of madhouse is this? I think shit show is the only proper description. A fucking wolf pack, in the middle of my town? Shit!"

"Billy, dear, Marcie can hear you," Felicity drawled in a low and raspy voice.

Billy leaned over his desk, holding his head in his hands. Ted looked around as if studying the ceiling was the most important way he could spend his day. The others looked elsewhere, too. Sue continued to glare at Ted.

When Billy lifted his head, he rubbed his temples. He was the mayor and had to do something to keep the peace.

"Ted," Billy said, snapping his fingers to get Ted's attention. "Since that's your pack, you need to get them under control. No more biting friends of the town. What do we call this place anyway?" Billy asked, distracting himself.

"I don't know. Chicago, North Chicago, Ohfuckistan," Timmons suggested. Felicity gave him the hairy eyeball. He looked away.

"North Chicago it is," Billy declared, slapping his hand on his desk. "If all decisions were so easy... Ted, where were we? Yes, you control that pack or they are out of here. We want them to stay, mind you, but they can't be biting Clyde, Aaron, or anyone else. Do you control where they hunt?"

"Yes," Ted replied, not committing to anything.

"They also patrol at night. We call them the wolf watch," Timmons added helpfully. Ted looked sideways at him.

Aaron rubbed his face. His black eye had come and gone while Billy was talking with them, but his face still hurt. He looked from person to person, but couldn't remember who hit him.

The wolf pack started howling and yipping. Ted raised one finger and ran outside. The pack was mobbing Terry Henry Walton since he carried a bucket brimming with fish. Char carried a laughing Kaeden. Terry was holding the bucket over his head as the wolves jumped at him.

"Ted!" he yelled when he saw the pack's alpha. Ted whistled and called to them.

"You see, every time we had fish in that bucket, they got fed. They're just a little anxious, you see. It hasn't been a good day," Ted said with his hands out, ready to take the bucket. Terry handed it over and Ted pulled a fish and handed it to the closest wolf. In rapid succession he gave a fish to each in his pack. Ten of Terry and Kae's hard-caught fish.

The boy wanted down, but Char wouldn't let him go. He wanted to pet the wolves. She'd let him later, when they weren't eating. Ted handed the bucket back, smiled, and went back into the base's main brick building.

Terry looked at his mostly empty bucket, rolled his eyes, and shook his head. Terry, Char, and Kae followed Ted inside, still carrying their bucket.

Billy stood when he saw Terry and Char on their way into the spacious office that was quickly filling. The smell of dog, fish, and Werewolf was almost too much. Felicity had her sleeve over her face.

"I guess we missed something," Char observed.

"Cats and dogs not getting along, dogs and dogs not getting along," Billy said, pointing to Clyde whimpering in Sue's arms. "But there is some good news!"

Terry couldn't imagine as he stroked Clyde's hair and examined his wounds. "Who bit my dog?" he asked dangerously.

"We're calling this place North Chicago!" Billy said, holding his hands up in triumph.

Clyde jumped from Sue's arms, stuffing his dog face into the bucket and grabbing a fish as he fell from Sue's arms. The bucket followed the dog down, spewing the remaining fish and snotty water on the floor. Clyde scrambled through the mess on his way out the door, holding his prize firmly in his jaws.

Terry turned to Sue as everyone looked at the mess on the floor. "Your dog made a mess," he told her, as he turned and walked briskly away.

❖ ❖ ❖

"You can't come through here," the man with the feathered headdress said in a deep voice.

Adams bristled, but relaxed and approached the man who was clearly in charge. "We are with Terry Henry Walton, bringing his herd to Chicago, for the good people of New Boulder."

"Welcome. We knew you were coming, but you can't come through here, because the village is right over that next rise. The cattle would probably do considerable damage. Please loop to the south and around, then leave your cattle to graze to the northeast on the shore of the river." Chief Foxtail smiled and waved to the others that he could see. "We invite you and all your people to be our guests for a celebration."

Adams smiled. "Thank you. I apologize for my misunderstanding. We happily accept your gracious invitation." Adams bowed to the chief.

"You are like the one called Charumati. We welcome all Were folk," the chief said, inclining his head slightly.

Adams closed his eyes and reached out with his senses. Hundreds of people nearby. Almost seventy head of cattle, horses, his people, and the chief before him. The air smelled of heat, sweat, and animals.

There had been a time when being a Werewolf was a secret. Now it seemed like everyone knew, and people were kind to them because of it. What a far different world it had become.

When Adams opened his eyes, the chief and his people had gone.

CHAPTER FIVE

When Mark returned for Mrs. Grimes, she was not happy. "What?" he asked.

"How long were you going to leave me out here, mister? Incompetent buffoons take that long to clean one little room!" she yelled at him, swinging at him with her wooden spoon-shaped walking stick. He dodged the deadly weapon and beckoned for her to follow.

She shuffled after him, climbed the stairs slowly, and walked into the vastly improved squad bay. Her room had been thoroughly cleaned and contained the two best pieces of furniture: a wobbly metal chair and a steel bunk with a mattress. They'd moved her meager personal items into the room.

"So, someone snuck around and ran to my room on the other side?" she wondered.

"It took them a while to find your stuff. Sorry for the

deceit, Mrs. Grimes. We want you to be comfortable," Mark said kindly. The rest of the platoon agreed and cheered for the old lady, making her blush.

"All right, cool your jets, people," she called, waving her arms for quiet. "Show me where the kitchen is in this place and then we'll see what we have to do."

Mark pursed his lips. No one moved.

"Don't tell me," she warned.

"There's no kitchen," Mark said, barely above whisper.

"I told you not to tell me!" she barked.

"There's a central mess and that's where everyone will eat until we get the food situation under control," Gerry said, stepping forward from the crowd. Kiwi held his hand in both of hers.

"And who are you, my lovely?" Mrs. Grimes asked.

"Kiwidinok of the Cheyenne," she said proudly, but in a small voice.

"Well, Kiwidinok, you are far too precious to be hanging out with this rabble. Let's see if we can find you better quarters. Mark?" Mrs. Grimes looked sternly at the sergeant.

"We have a room, right behind the power plant. That's where we've been staying since we got here," Gerry replied.

"You're moving in here with the rest of us," Mark said flatly.

"Poppycock!" Mrs. Grimes yelled. "That young lady is not moving in here. She's not a member of the FDG." Mrs. Grimes jutted her chin as she looked up at the sergeant.

"But Private Geronimo is," Mark argued.

"Where's Blackbeard?" the old woman asked.

"Well, he's with Hank, but he's not far!"

Mrs. Grimes chewed her cheek as she engaged Mark in a stare-down. The two squads that made up the platoon circled them like they were watching a prize fight.

"Dammit!" Mark cried. "Mrs. Grimes, I'm the sergeant and I'm supposed to be in charge."

"Yes, dear, you go on thinking that. Mr. Grimes thought he was in charge too, bless his departed soul."

"I'll talk with the colonel and see what we can work out. Gerry, are there any quarters closer to chow?" Mark asked. Mrs. Grimes huffed. She hated the idea of her cooking being called chow.

"There is, but just like the rest of the base, it's trashed. Well, this is just the empty shell of a building. At least over there, it's a series of single rooms," Gerry told them. No matter where they went, it would be work to get the rooms ready, but they had eighteen people. Everything was easier with more hands to help.

"Sounds like we're moving, Mrs. Grimes!" Mark declared to a chorus of cheers. "First squad, bring her stuff, and that includes the bed. Meet me out front in one minute. MOVE!"

Mark crooked an elbow for Mrs. Grimes to hold as they descended the stairs. "It has turned into a lovely day, don't you think?" Mark asked the old woman.

❖ ❖ ❖

Sue petted Clyde's head while Ted rubbed her back. Shonna and Merrit stood side by side, holding hands and trying to look innocent. Timmons had his arms crossed. Aaron shuffled his feet nervously while Char glared at them all. Terry stood to the side leaning against the railcar on which the Mini Cooper gleamed. Kaeden stood on the platform behind him.

She walked slowly in front of the group, back and forth,

looking at each before moving to the next, then back again.

"Who started it?" she demanded, smacking her fist into her palm.

"I think maybe my pack might have, possibly," Ted stammered.

"You're not making your point, Ted. I love the boat, by the way," she said.

He brightened up.

"Get your pack under control!" she yelled at his face. He ducked his head and winced as if he was going to be hit. She gripped his shoulder firmly, but in the way of a friend and not an enemy.

"And what were you stupid fuckers doing when all that was going on?" Char wondered, looking sternly at Timmons. "You're the beta, how did you let this happen?"

"He's a fucking cat!" Timmons blurted. Char grabbed his shirt collar and pulled him down to her level.

"I don't care," she whispered. "Aaron!" Char yelled. The man jumped. "Don't bite Ted or any of these people or the wolves, do you understand?"

"I'll try my best, but I'm pretty sure I can't guarantee anything."

"Shut up," she said and he returned to looking at his big feet. "I only have one pack, and you are all in it, do you understand me?"

The Werewolves grumbled and the Were-tiger whined. Char clenched her fists as she rolled her eyes, breathing deeply to help her avoid beating everyone who was standing there.

"A fucking bear?" Timmons asked, looking at the big shaggy creature running toward them.

"That's Hank, our grizzly. Blackie shouldn't be far behind.

They're going with us, all of us, tomorrow when we introduce ourselves to that Were-bear. Maybe that guy will see a kindred spirit in Hank and decide that we're not such bad people," Terry suggested, eyebrows raised and grinning.

Shonna, Merrit, and Sue had spent enough time with the bear cub that they didn't think anything about it. They looked at him as the big goofy cousin who breaks your toys whenever he visits.

Timmons leaned sideways to get a better look at the animal who decided to stop, then turned and dashed into the woods along the side of the road. Blackie strolled down the road, watching. He shrugged and continued to the group. The wolf pack sniffed as Blackbeard approached, but stayed where they were.

"Aaron, I need you to pet each of the wolves," Terry said. "Same for you, Corporal.

"I'm not sure that's a good idea," Ted said, standing protectively in front of the pack.

"Well then, Ted, what do you suggest we do to expedite the integration of the pack with the rest of our mob?" Terry countered.

"I'll introduce them one by one." Ted talked with the former alpha male, then grabbed him by the scruff of his neck to help move him out front.

"Aaron, you first. Corporal Blackbeard, then you, and get Hank up here, too," Terry told them.

The wolf growled at Aaron, but the tall man took a knee and held his hand out, palm up. The wolf sniffed as Ted stroked his head and ruffled his ears. The wolf looked back at the pack and growled. The rest of them joined him to sniff Aaron and Blackie. They seemed to have no problem with the human who smelled like a bear.

Ted had to slap a few wolf heads before he was comfortable that the pack had accepted the Were-tiger.

"Now change into your Were form," Terry ordered.

"Please, I would prefer not." Aaron started to slowly step away. Terry intercepted him.

"I'm pretty sure that wasn't open for debate. I can't have a cat fight if we're in the middle of the shit. I need to know that everyone is going to work together, so go on now and change." Terry waited. The man stood straight up, then disappeared into his clothes, where a great tiger emerged. Sleek, orange with black stripes. Pale yellow eyes looked at the group. The cat crouched and then leapt sideways, landing softly on the platform next to Kaeden.

Char gasped and started to run, but there was no time. Aaron lowered his head and bumped Kaeden, who seemed completely unafraid of the predators that surrounded him. Terry held out a hand to stop Char as he slowly approached the great cat.

Kaeden gripped Aaron's ears as they held their foreheads together. "I want to be a tiger, too!" Kae called out. Char picked up Aaron's clothes and tossed them on the platform.

The wolf pack remained wary, hunched and watching every one of the Were-tiger's moves.

Hank ambled onto the road, roaring his disapproval of something. Blackie met the bear and calmed him. Together they joined the pack. Hank sniffed tentatively, then stood on his back legs and roared again.

The cub was growing up. Terry wondered when they would no longer be able to control him. The pack backed up, baring fangs as they went. The cat snarled from the platform and crouched to leap. Kae threw himself around the tiger's neck and spoke into his hairy ear. Aaron settled down on the platform, lying down and tucking his front paws under his chest.

Hank dropped to the ground, bumped Blackie, and rolled to his back to get his belly scratched.

When they turned back, Aaron was putting his clothes on.

"Everything was okay?" he asked. "Since there's no blood, I'm assuming..."

Terry slapped him in the leg and smiled. "You are his manny," Terry said, pointing to Kaeden.

"Huh? What's a manny?" he wondered. Char looked at Terry with the same expression on her face.

"Male nanny. Welcome to the family, Aaron."

"But what if..." Aaron often let his thoughts taper off. Being alone had done that to him. He wasn't used to being around so many people. Not yet anyway, and Terry was giving him no choice but to figure it out.

"What if you don't want to?" Terry asked. "Don't make me reach up there and punch you in the kneecap!"

Kaeden held his hands out, and the tall man picked the boy up. "Wow, I can see the end of the world from up here!"

❖ ❖ ❖

When they had the cattle settled outside the village, Adams asked everyone to use the river to clean up. It was the only time the group would be guests at someone else's home, and he wanted to put on a good face for the chief and his people.

Boris refused to leave his weapons behind. Adams was insistent and they agreed to disagree. Adams ordered Boris and his squad to remain behind and watch over the cattle.

"Rather miss dinner than be unarmed," Boris replied snottily.

Adams couldn't let it go.

"Why are you with us?" he asked.

"To defend this group and the cattle from any enemies we may find along the way, hunt for food, and most importantly, see that you get to Chicago," Boris said, hearing his own words making Adams's argument.

"We're going to be over there and we're not taking weapons, so do what you have to do, but I wouldn't want to be you facing Terry Henry Walton if you lost people." Adams stalked away.

In the end, Boris left one man behind to watch their stack of rifles and the cattle, while the other six joined the group heading to the village.

The chief and a small delegation were waiting for them on the hill. Adams met him and the two men shook hands. Foxtail greeted the Werewolf as an old friend, draping an arm over his shoulder as they walked together toward the village, where a bonfire occupied the empty space between the tents. The smell of roasting buffalo filled the air.

The natives stood on one side of the fire while the people from New Boulder stood on the other in uncomfortable silence. It seemed like a standoff, or a game of Red Rover, where someone would run from one side to the other and try to break through the line.

Adams snickered.

Chief Foxtail tapped his staff to get everyone's attention. It was already quiet except for the crackling of the fire and the movements of the two people tending it.

"We welcome our brothers from the south and wish them well on their journey," the chief said, projecting his voice for all to hear. "We have communed with Mother Earth and she has told us that this land will be consumed by dust and heat, and that we must move. Tomorrow, my people, we will join the brave souls here in a journey to our new home!"

Adams stood dumbfounded.

"I'm glad I didn't miss this," Boris said, after having found his way next to the Werewolf.

CHAPTER SIX

"What's going to happen to us, Geronimo?" Kiwi asked.

"We do as we have been doing, make this a better and better place, turn it back into civilization," Gerry parroted.

"I don't know what that word means—civilization. Everything I knew about a town was from our village by the river. That's where I was born and raised. This is so different," she sighed, gripping his hand so tightly that it cut off the circulation to his fingers.

They started to throb.

He pried her fingers away to stand up and face her. "What do you want, Kiwi?"

"I'd like to have a purpose," Kiwi said, looking at a spot on Gerry's shirt. "It seems that I'm in the way, a backpack that you carry, something that you'll come home to. That Mark guy is pushing me to join the Force, it seems, and I'm not sure I want that."

"Let's talk with the colonel and the major, maybe your grandmother?" Gerry suggested, stroking the side of her face with one hand. She was in pain and he didn't know what to do. His heart melted seeing the sadness in her dark brown eyes. "Right now. We'll find them and talk with them right now."

Kiwi seemed to perk up at having something to do. Gerry found Mark first to tell him that they needed to talk with the colonel.

"Why don't you think you can tell me?" Mark said, more harshly than he intended.

"This is a civilian issue. It's not tied to the Force. We just need to talk with him, which is something he's always told us. Come see me, he said. That's what we want to do," Gerry replied.

"Then I'm going with you," Mark declared. He yelled at Jim and Ivan to keep preparing the barracks and that he'd return soon.

Kiwi was anxious, refusing to talk as they walked. Gerry felt like he was being marched to his own funeral. His heart was in his throat and Kiwi felt no better.

But the sergeant knew where the colonel and the major were. He made a beeline for them and the eternal walk took only five minutes. They found them on the tracks outside the base with the rest of the Werewolves, their boy, the tall new-comer, Blackbeard, and Hank.

They stopped when they were a respectful distance away.

"Sergeant, Corporal, come on, we were just finishing up," Terry called, waving them to him.

"Tomorrow morning, first light, meet us in front of the

mayor's building," Char reminded them. Ted swung wide around Hank with the wolf pack loping close behind. Timmons tipped his chin and smiled as he walked past Gerry and Kiwi. He'd never forget that those two saved his life.

The others meandered away. Aaron remained standing on the platform. "Well?" Char asked him.

He held his hands out, palms up in a sign of confusion.

"If you would be so kind, take Kae for a walk around the base, introduce yourselves to the good people who are working their asses off to build us a city while you stand around picking your nose." Char pointed toward the base.

Aaron climbed down slowly, hanging on to Kaeden with one hand.

"You need to show Aaron around, see what everyone is doing and help where you can, okay, sweetheart?" Char asked the little boy. He nodded and tapped Aaron's head to signal that he was ready to go. Kae started talking to the tall man the second they walked away.

Terry and Char's hands intertwined of their own accord as they watched the two walking away. The tall man seemed to have a new spring in his step. "It's not that I don't trust Hank, but he's a wild animal. I prefer a Were-tiger as the guardian of our son, and they both seem happy with the arrangement," Terry whispered.

Gerry waved at Blackie as they passed. "We need to catch up, wild man!" Gerry called with a laugh. They'd been chosen together as the second group to join the Force de Guerre. They were both small and seemed out of place, but they'd each made their mark in a significant way that belied their size.

Kiwi stopped to scratch the bear's head, then ran to catch up. Blackie and Hank watched for a moment, then strolled the other way.

Mark and Gerry saluted as they approached.

Gerry made to speak, but Mark cut him off. "He says they want to see you and won't tell me what it's about," he said abruptly.

"Well now, isn't that a mouthful," Char interjected, crossing her arms as she saw Mark's position as interference.

"Corporal Geronimo, are you here to bitch about the sergeant?" Terry asked.

"No, sir, not at all," Gerry replied.

"Good. Sergeant, you are dismissed," Terry directed. Mark looked confused for a second. Terry narrowed his eyes and clenched his jaw.

Obeying orders was something that Terry drilled constantly into the discipline of the Force. Mark was too slow. Terry grabbed the sergeant's uniform collar and pulled him forward. "I think I gave you a fucking order," Terry growled.

"Yes, sir!" Mark stepped back, saluted, and jogged away.

Terry turned to the young couple holding hands. "This is new," he blurted out, earning him a slap across the arm from his wife.

"We don't know what to do," Gerry stumbled, then looked to Kiwi for help.

"What's my position?" she asked.

Terry's mind raced through a series of crude jokes, but this was serious and he respected them both too much to make jokes at their expense. He thought for a moment and decided it deserved a longer explanation.

"Back in the days of the Corps, many of my folks were married. Dependent wives, they called them. Isn't that some crap, huh?" Terry shook his head. "Good people ripped from their homes and moved into some cracker box base housing where shortly thereafter, their husbands were deployed, leaving them alone without friends or family. Then every three years, we moved them, so they could go through it all over again."

He had their focus. They leaned toward him so they wouldn't miss a word.

"We have a chance to do better this time. We have the Force living side by side with the civilians we've sworn to protect. We're all here together, but what about you, Miss Kiwidinok? Everyone needs to have a purpose, a chance to fulfill their own destiny. I have to ask, what is yours?"

Kiwi was still young and hadn't figured out what she wanted to be when she grew up.

"I love the horses and the open range. I love my native traditions, too," she said in a small voice. They waited, because she wasn't finished.

"I know that my grandfather gave me to Gerry to be his wife. I'm not property, but my grandfather knows that. He saw the bond that we would develop. I hope that he is happy with the path that we follow."

Terry and Char looked at each other in surprise.

"Have you had no time to talk with your grandmother since our arrival?" Terry asked. She shook her head.

"First order of business, you two go see your family. The major and I will find you quarters somewhere between the barracks and your family, because you deserve to have access to both worlds since they overlap. It's not my place to tear you from one and throw you into the other," Terry said softly, looking at them both with pride.

"We need a horse master who's not in the FDG. Do you want the job, Kiwi?" Char asked. The young girl nodded, but never let go of Gerry's hand.

"It's settled then. Make sure you let Mark know what

we've talked about. I need him comfortable with what everyone is doing, that there's no subterfuge." Terry nodded to them as Gerry saluted while still holding Kiwi's hand. Terry had a hard time not correcting him.

"By the way, are you two going to get married?" Char asked innocently.

The youngsters looked at each other, smiling, and both nodded when they turned back to Char.

"Here's what you're going to do," Char said. Gerry looked at the colonel. "Don't look at him, you need to look at me, he doesn't know anything about romance." Gerry turned back to Char. "You are going to ask Kiwi's grandmother for her hand in marriage. If she approves, you're both going to see Billy, get your names written in his book, and you're going to ask him for the town's blessing with a celebration. Antioch can do the formal thing like he did for us, if that's what you'd like, or you can come up with a ceremony based on your personal beliefs."

Char ran her hand up Terry's back as she spoke and he could only think of their ceremony and what it had done for them.

"What you decide to do will be the standard for everyone who follows. Keep that in mind. You could be starting a new tradition that we'll look back, centuries from now, and wonder why we're doing things the way we do," Terry said.

Without another word, the couple walked away, chatting excitedly.

"Well done, my husband," Char started. "That dependent thing chapped my ass. I'm glad I wasn't the only one."

"Young Marines in love. Divorce rate was through the roof. Commitment to the Corps, just like the commitment to the Force de Guerre. I told Charlie that he didn't get to stay in New Boulder when that's what he wanted. I'm already that guy, the one who rules with an iron fist over other people's lives. Am I doing the right thing, Char?" Terry asked.

She didn't answer with words, but the warmth of her kiss told him that he had her approval, which he needed as much as his own. When they separated, he looked at her sparkling purple eyes. "I could get lost in there forever."

"I won't forget you said that, when our daughter has kept you awake for two weeks straight," she replied slyly.

"Daughter?" he asked. She nodded indifferently. "Two weeks, what?"

"Oh, you didn't know? Werewolf pups are notorious for sleeping fifteen minutes and then being up for three hours. Shall we?" she said as she walked toward the base.

❖ ❖ ❖

"What do we do with the Mini Cooper now that we have it?" Timmons asked. Ted stroked his chin thoughtfully.

"It'll take everything we have to haul it down here, or we take it up the tracks to the old power plant and we bring it up, with as much of the grid as we can manage. We use this plant to provide power to bring the other plant up," Ted said conversationally.

"We don't turn the lights on here until we can turn on all the lights?" Timmons asked.

"Unless we can move enough fuel to make it a non-issue," Ted replied, which changed his original argument.

"Sometimes, I really hate you, Ted," Timmons answered, leaving Ted standing on the shore.

They had been going to the plant every single day and puttering around, but everything they needed to keep it operational was outside the plant. Fuel and water. The one time they had it running, they had used the pump to fill the water tank outside the facility. The previous time, they had manually filled the boiler. That had taken a great deal of time and effort.

They needed power to make power. Timmons was still amazed at the logic failure within the system. It didn't have a manual backup, but they'd worked around it. With five people, he could bring the plant to life within an hour.

For the long-term goal, all he needed was a power line running from the small plant directly to the larger facility a mile up the coast. Power to make power.

"Ted!" Timmons yelled. "We have work to do!"

When Timmons went outside, he saw the sail as Ted maneuvered his boat out of the small harbor.

"Never mind, I'll take care of it," Timmons said to Ted's retreating form. Ted waved one hand, while keeping the other on the tiller.

"We have a shit pot of people here, and here I am working on this bastard all by myself. Isn't that a total bitch?" Timmons told no one as he rolled up his sleeves and headed for the enclosure containing the distribution transformers.

❖ ❖ ❖

"You don't have to ask me for her hand in marriage, my boy. Black Feather granted that before his death," Autumn Dawn told him following his bold but stumbling request for Kiwi's hand in marriage.

"What? Grandfather is dead?" Kiwi asked.

"Yes, dear, I'm sorry that we haven't had a chance to talk," the old lady said slowly, without any hint of sadness at her loss. "It was a couple months ago. Terry and Char were there. He suffered all that time waiting for them so he could say just four words."

"I am sorry in that I didn't come to visit sooner," the young woman replied, kneeling at her grandmother's feet.

"It is okay, but I wish you would visit more often." The old woman patted Kiwi on the head. Gerry had never met the grandfather since he'd stayed with the horses when the others joined the chief.

Gerry was on the outside looking in then as he was now. "What four words?" he asked.

"One land, one people," she replied in a soft voice.

Rapids and Winter Rain were nowhere to be seen. Geronimo felt like leaving. He thought that Kiwi wanted time alone with her grandmother, but he hadn't asked and he didn't know for sure. He moved one foot toward the door and Kiwi looked up. "Where are you going?" she asked.

Gerry tried to act casual as if he hadn't been ready to run away screaming. He shrugged indifferently. Autumn Dawn started to laugh, making a dry raspy sound that ended in a cough. "Go see the mayor, do what you need to do, and then come back to me, and we'll talk about the long road from there to here."

Kiwi kissed her grandmother on the cheek and grabbed Gerry's hand as she ran out the door, dragging him with her.

Autumn Dawn clapped her hands together and closed her eyes. "It's everything you hoped for, my husband…"

CHAPTER SEVEN

Terry, Char, and Kae met the pack at sunrise. The platoon was there, too. Aaron stood nearly a head taller than everyone else, even though he tried to blend in with a wall in the back. Kae found him and was immediately picked up.

Hank ambled about, tearing up a bush that was growing out of control next to the mayor's building.

Terry thought about calling it town hall, but wasn't a fan of previous government titles. He would encourage them to call it something unique to the community they were building.

"Well?" Sue asked. Char glared at her for only a moment until they heard the rumble of approaching vehicles.

"No need to walk if we don't have to," Terry declared.

Sue relaxed. "I admit, that was worth the wait. I'm not in a hurry to strain this body." She stretched and turned under the watchful gaze of every single man in the platoon.

"Kiwi, what are you doing here?" Terry asked when he saw the young woman peeking out from behind Gerry. "We're not riding the horses."

Timmons raised a hand and stepped forward. "I asked her to come. She senses things that we don't. I think you should draft her. Put her out front with Sue to see all the evil demons before they jump out of the dark." Timmons nodded vigorously. Sue took one step and punched him in the shoulder hard enough to make him stagger.

First Sergeant Blevin stopped the bus and popped the door open. "All aboard!" he yelled. A truck pulled up behind the bus and the dune buggy maneuvered from behind the truck. Corporal Heitz stopped it and hopped out.

It was the undamaged buggy with the fifty cal on top.

"I'd throw you the keys, sir, but it ain't got none of those," the corporal announced.

"At ease, Corporal. You have delivered unto me mana from heaven." Terry shook the old man's hand, then man-hugged him, before climbing aboard and running the mod deuce through a function check. The platoon climbed aboard the bus. They were geared up in camouflaged uniforms, flak jackets, and helmets. Everyone was armed with an AK-47 rifle.

Ted stood there confused as the pack loaded into the back of the truck. Aaron and Kae climbed aboard the bus with Blackie and Hank. The wolf pack stood there, unsure of what to do.

"Leave them here," Terry called. Ted looked at Terry as if he were insane, then pointed to the wolves.

Terry closed his eyes and wished that when he opened them back up, the problem would be solved. He slowly counted to five.

When he opened his eyes, he found that Char had climbed into the driver's seat and Ted was still looking at him. Neither he nor his wolf pack had moved.

"Just put them in the back of the truck," Terry snapped, climbing from the dune buggy to help. Ted and Terry each picked up a wolf and put them into the back. The vicious predators were shaking.

"They've never ridden before. What if they get car sick?" Terry didn't dignify that with an answer. He heard a yip as he put the next wolf in. Sue was sitting up front, holding Clyde in her lap.

Incrementally, they piled the wolves into the back of the five-ton. Terry shut the gate after all were in and then assumed his rightful position in the passenger seat of the dune buggy. He looked at Char. She shrugged one shoulder.

"I'm not firing that thing, so that leaves you, Bwana the Great White Hunter. Man the mod deuce! Rounds down range!" Char yelled, waving her hands around.

"I don't wave my hands around like that when I'm making man talk," he said in his deepest voice. Then changed back. "Did you see Clyde's up front? Where did he come from?"

"Probably his mother with a litter of other puppies," Char answered, putting the dune buggy in gear and easing in front of the truck. She started slowly until she was sure the other vehicles were following. Then she picked up speed.

"Is anyone taking this shit seriously?" Terry complained.

"One Were-bear. One. And we have enough firepower to level a city. It's hard to take that seriously." Char shook her head as she drove.

"You know that you would look perfect behind the wheel if we could find you some sunglasses," Terry said, admiring his wife's profile.

"I don't look perfect now?" she parried.

Terry knew he was cornered. There was no way out. "There are shades of perfect…" But he couldn't sound convincing.

"Uh-huh," she said, mentally tallying one on her side of their endless board.

Char was keeping it at twenty-five miles an hour. The cool morning air made for a pleasant drive. The truck and bus were rolling along easily behind.

"Baby names?" he asked.

"Do you have anything in mind?" Char wondered.

"No. We could go classic, like Shakespeare or Ancient Greece, maybe Sanskrit akin to your name, whatever. The sky's the limit." Terry searched his mind for something he liked, but kept returning to Melissa. He couldn't do that to Char or himself. There was only one Melissa.

"How about Bill?" Char asked.

"For a girl?"

"You said the sky was the limit, and now you're saying there's a limit. I swear, TH, just when I thought I had you figured out," Char prodded him.

"Girl's names, not just any baby's name, but if you want to call her Bill, that's your business. That's not going to be her official name. So there." Terry slapped the dash as if physically driving his point home.

"Official name. What does that mean in this day and age?" Char wondered.

"That's a good question, lover. How about, what we call her when she's in trouble?" Terry offered.

"Now that is something I can get behind. That's a good limit, TH. You are momentarily redeemed. Hang on," she said as she waved an arm out the top of the buggy and pointed to the right. She took the next turn and headed toward the lake.

They hadn't driven this road before, but the sun was up and shining and the road wasn't blocked. They maneuvered between numerous dead vehicles and had to stop once to let the five-ton bounce a rusted wreck out of the way.

"Not far now, TH. You might want to man the gun."

Terry unbuckled himself and climbed into position, leaning over the roll bar with the fifty cal pulled tightly into his shoulder. It was his power stance. He felt both exposed and invincible at the same time.

Char pulled up to a nondescript house and shut the buggy off. "He's in there."

"What?" Terry exclaimed. His choice would have to been to stop farther away and plan their attack. Here they were, on top of the objective. He found himself having to plan the attack on the fly, but Char was right in one thing. They had enough firepower to level a city.

The bus door opened and as usual, Hank was the first one out. He rumbled straight for the house with Blackie close in pursuit. Kae was hot on his heels, with Aaron running after him.

"Grab that boy!" Terry screamed, furious as the situation rapidly spiraled out of control. "Firing positions there and there!"

Terry pointed with his arm past the dune buggy to the front and then made a second slashing motion to the right side of the house.

Clyde started barking and the wolf pack ran past on their way after something up the street.

Aaron caught Kaeden and hauled him into the air, jogging back to the dune buggy.

"You stay behind the buggy, do you understand me?"

Terry growled. The boy started to cry. Char gave Terry the unhappy look again.

Terry climbed out and kneeled next to Kae. The Werewolves moved into a position between the buggy and the house. They watched closely because they knew the Werebear was inside.

"I don't want you to get hurt," Terry told the little boy. "I need you to stay back here in case there's a fight. I don't know what I'd do if anything happened to you. Aaron?"

The Were-tiger nodded. "I've got him. With a bear in there, I'm good back here."

Terry pulled his bullwhip and walked into the overgrown front yard. "For fuck's sake, you know we're out here. Come on out," Terry called.

"You kiss mother with potty mouth?" a booming voice said from inside the small house. Hank was standing with paws against the door.

"We just want to talk with you," Terry replied.

"Up your ass sideways without soap!" the voice bellowed. Terry snapped his whip and loosened his shoulders. He'd never seen a Were-bear before, but he had an overwhelming urge to kick its ass.

"Move stinky dick away from door. I come out," the voice called through a broken window.

"Come on, Hank! Give the man some room," Blackie yelled. The two wrestled briefly before Hank ambled toward Terry.

The bear didn't slow down and Terry ended up diving out of the way, rolling and coming back to his feet, to find a huge man standing in the doorway, chuckling to himself. His shock of dark brown hair was messed, his face covered with stubble and his heavy eyebrows cast dark shadows over his eyes.

He wore barely more than rags.

His disheveled appearance didn't detract from his well-muscled physique. He was bigger than Marcus, looking like a professional wrestler of old.

"My name is Terry Henry Walton, Colonel from the Force de Guerre. We only want one thing, to make sure that our settlement is left in peace." Terry decided that he needed to work on his speech.

"Maybe I want to live in peace. What fuck did I do to get War Force here, damaging my calm," the Were-bear asked in his heavy Russian accent.

Terry coiled his whip and strapped it to his belt.

"Valid points all. What's your name, friend?"

"Yevgeniy Stalin, Eugene, man of steel. You call me Gene, little man, but none of rest of you. You call me Mr. Stalin." Gene swept an arm to take in the rest of the pack and both squads aiming their rifles.

"Stand down," Terry called as Hank ran past him toward the Were-bear. Gene crouched and Hank jumped. The big man caught the two-hundred-pound bear and cradled him in his arms like a baby. The grizzly cub made odd noises and Gene talked back with him. In the bear world, a male wouldn't hesitate to kill a male cub, even his own. All males were challengers.

It was good to see that the Were-bear had evolved beyond that. Blackie stood beside Terry, mortified.

"He's not your bear, son," Terry said softly.

"Okay, but we change name. Hank no good. He look like Bogdan to me. I call him Bogdan. Okay, I come, too. I come with you, Bogdan, teach you how to be real bear," the massive man cooed to the grizzly cub.

"Wait, what? What in the holy jump the fuck up and

down just happened?" Terry asked Char as he had a nearly overwhelming desire to shoot someone. He turned back to the Were-bear.

"What did you do in Russia? What was your trade?" Terry asked, blocking Gene from going to the bus which was parked far too close for Terry's comfort.

"I was all Army wrestler. Won Olympic medal. Then back to my job as nuclear weapons specialist," Gene said proudly.

"No shit," Terry mumbled.

Ted leaned closer. "I'm a nuclear engineer," he said softly.

"Fuck off! You are tiny like flea," Gene boomed again, then laughed. "Yes, tiny, we talk good about neutron bomb, no?"

Gene balanced Hank in one arm as he reached an immense hand out and slapped Ted on the back hard enough to knock him down.

The two squads from the Force stepped away from the Were-bear as he strolled past, up the steps and into the bus, still carrying the grizzly cub.

Terry's nostrils flared as he tried to maintain the last shred of his dignity. "Sergeant, get the men on the bus."

Mark hesitated, but the glare from the colonel galvanized him into action. He started yelling and pushing. There was a mad rush for the bus and they filled it from the front to the back. Blackie walked boldly up the stairs and joined Gene and Hank in the back.

The pack loaded the wolves into the truck, then climbed in themselves. Sue whistled for Clyde, who appeared out of nowhere, chewing on something. James, Lacy, Gerry, Kiwi, Aaron, and Kae were last getting on the bus. Char stopped Kae and made him get in the dune buggy instead. The others took seats in the back by Gene and Hank/Bogdan.

Terry looked at Char, hoping that her purple eyes would cheer him up. It didn't help.

"My head hurts," he admitted.

"This day just got a whole lot more interesting, don't you think, dear?" Char asked, eyes sparkling radiantly as her voice turned sultry. "I'm sorry you didn't get to shoot anything with your big gun. Maybe next time."

"Maybe," Terry replied as he vigorously rubbed his temples.

CHAPTER EIGHT

The natives were stalwart as they powered forward, keeping up with the cattle. Adams was walking, as were the FDG squad. The carts had been filled with necessities and the old and the young rode on the horses. The village had produced twenty-seven horses of their own, but they had nearly one hundred and fifty people with a broad age disparity, from seven weeks to seventy years.

The people capable of walking were walking, and Adams pushed them all, keeping everyone moving.

He wasn't happy about the latest development. Terry and Char wouldn't be expecting such an influx of people, but the chief's presence was calming.

Adams was responsible and ran back and forth to talk with one person or another, but he found himself returning to the chief's side each time.

"Why didn't you go with Terry and Char when they came

through last time?" Adams finally summoned the courage to ask.

"It wasn't our time, yet, and their loud vehicles were filled. We would have held them back. No, it was our plan all along to wait for you," Foxtail said matter-of-factly.

"Did they know you were going to join us?" Adams questioned.

"No." The chief looked serenely ahead then scanned the horizons. "A storm is coming. I think we had best find shelter. There are ruins up ahead that we can use. I suggest we run." Without waiting, the chief whooped and started running. His people ran with him. The horses kicked into a trot, then a canter, then a gallop as they drove the panicking cattle.

One cart hit a bump and overturned. The driver was barely able to crawl out of the way before the stampede destroyed the cart and everything in it. Someone ran up to help the man unhook the terrified horse, holding the reins to keep it from bolting.

Boris and a couple others from the FDG recovered their horses and rode after the cattle, hoping to turn them toward the ruins before the storm hit.

The people ran as if they were being chased by the hounds of hell. The first thirty people into the ruins were in better shape and they funneled people to the buildings with roofs intact, with basements free from dirt. The cattle had to shelter behind walls, because there was no space indoors for them. Boris, Everett, Hayden, the Weathers boys, and others circled the cattle to keep them from straying too far into the quickening breeze. The people wrapped scarves around their faces and ducked their heads while they waited for the storm to hit.

❖ ❖ ❖

"A what?" Billy asked, not completely surprised at yet another creature being added to the menagerie that seemed to be tied to anything Terry Henry Walton touched.

"A Were-bear. They come from Russia, so his accent is a little thick, but he seems nice and Hank likes him, although Gene insists the grizzly's name is now Bogdan, for what it's worth."

Billy had no answer to that. Why couldn't there be a simple fight between two farmers? He longed for the good old days when that was the extent of an exciting day.

"Before we bring him in, there's probably one other thing you should know," Terry said, waiting for an acknowledgement from Billy. The mayor rolled his finger at Terry.

"We have a truce with a Vampire who lives in the city. He says he'll work for me if we don't kill him. In return, he won't feed on any of our people. Should I bring Gene in now?"

Billy didn't skip a beat. "Yes, that's fine, bring in this Were-bear of yours."

Terry got up and walked out.

"What the hell?" Terry yelled from out front.

"Fuck off, he comes," someone bellowed in a heavy Russian accent. The grizzly cub formerly known as Hank dragged his claws across the marble in the entryway. Heavy footfalls signaled the arrival of the Were-bear called Gene. He had a handful of the cub's fur and was dragging him backwards toward the office.

He ducked and turned sideways as he came through the doorway and with one final yank, deposited the whining grizzly cub on the floor in the middle of the office.

Felicity tried to crawl backwards through the wall. Marcie

started crying. Billy sat slack-jawed.

"I am Yevgenniy Stalin. You call me Gene." The big man's voice reverberated within the mayor's office.

Billy hadn't thought of the room as small until the Were-bear and his mini-me arrived.

"Terry?" Billy inquired casually, wondering about where Terry Henry Walton had disappeared. *That fucker bailed on me after dumping this steaming mess in my office.* Billy Spires, Mayor of North Chicago, recovered quickly.

"Nice to meet you, Gene. What can I do for you?" Billy asked, smiling pleasantly while on the inside he was both furious and terrified.

"I want to see Mini Cooper," Gene demanded, smacking a fist on the desk. Billy swore that the whole room shook.

"I'll leave that to Terry Henry Walton and Ted, who is responsible for the reactor. I'm sure they'll be accommodating. Will that be all?" Billy stood, trying to signal that the meeting was over.

"Where will Bogdan and I live?" the man asked, more quietly. "I don't like to be near people, you see. Maybe we live in suburbs of your town?"

Billy saw the sincerity in his eyes.

"I'll see to that personally. Stop by here later and I'm sure I'll have something for you. The homes are a little trashed and it may need some work, but it'll be what you want." Billy saw the spark of humanity and wanted to help.

Then it was gone when the man stood up and growled at the grizzly cub to get it moving out the door. The bear formerly known as Hank slid his way across the marble as he made for the door.

Gene didn't wave or say goodbye, he simply left, ducking and angling his way through the too-small doorway. Billy turned in time to see Felicity wrinkling her nose.

He moved around his desk to the doorway and stood in it, comparing his own size to that of the man who had just left. Billy turned one way then the other.

"Hmmm," he mumbled. "I guess we shouldn't make him mad."

❖ ❖ ❖

"No!" Ted said.

"Just for a little bit, Ted. I really need to clear my head," Terry begged.

"You left fish blood all over it last time. It wasn't better than when you took it, so you don't get to borrow it ever again," Ted stated definitively, stomping his foot and thrusting his chin out.

"I thought I cleaned it pretty well," Terry answered.

"There was a bloody handprint on the port rail!"

"That's your definition of all over?" Terry replied.

"You can't borrow it." Ted strutted toward the dock.

Terry had learned a great deal about their resident genius. "You'd rather sink it than let me borrow it, wouldn't you, Ted?" Terry called after the man.

"You got that right," Ted said over his shoulder.

Char and Kae were on the beach, climbing on the rocks, watching Terry crash and burn.

"You don't get to run off and play every time there's something going on that you don't like," she said conversationally. He didn't take offense.

"I want to give things time to shake out, and I think Kae liked fishing. Didn't you, buddy?"

"It was okay," the little man replied. He was bummed that

Hank and Blackie weren't together anymore.

Blackbeard was devastated.

But Kae liked both Aaron and Gene, the latest additions to the pack. Terry needed to give things time to shake out, let people find their way.

"I know what I've been missing," Terry decided. "Training. Combat training. We've been on the road too long, engaged in world building, when we need to step back, find our roots, and then branch out. How can we keep the people safe if we can't fight? I've done your pack a disservice. Tomorrow morning, when Joseph shows up, day one of our new training regimen begins."

Terry and Char sparred every single day, but they pulled their punches, so even they were slowing down. Terry couldn't strike his lover and Char learned that she couldn't either. Their moves became more like a dance than an all-out wail fest, Terry's preferred fighting technique that he demonstrated on the Forsaken.

"There's a marina right up the coast. Let's take a look-see and then we have some people we need to talk with." Terry helped his family out of the rocks and together they walked north.

The Waukegan Harbor and Marina was nearly two miles away, sitting next to the old power plant.

"I have yet to get a straight answer from Ted on what he's going to do with that nuclear reactor," Terry said, enjoying the breeze and the lake air. Humidity in the air was refreshing after the desert-like conditions they'd survived and traveled through.

"I'm sure Ted has something in mind. I think he's in love with that reactor. It was the latest technology before the fall." Char squinted into the distance. An overgrown path followed the shoreline for as far as she could see.

"Who would have thought that we'd call Chicago a paradise?" Terry wondered.

"I'm not calling it that," Char countered. "I'll commit to calling it nicer than the last place we were, but paradise? That sounded like Cancun, according to the pack. Too bad it's on the other side of hell."

"Does the Mississippi still flow?" Terry asked rhetorically. They'd crossed it in Minnesota and it was as robust as ever. "Maybe the locks and dams are gooned up, but with a small boat, I expect we could make it to New Orleans, then across the Gulf of Mexico. It wouldn't be any harder than moving a town from Colorado to here."

"Then what?" Char prompted.

"Then we'd be stuck down there." Terry fingered the communicator in his pocket. He imagined a conversation with Akio, begging him for a ride back to Chicago in the pod. Terry expected that it wouldn't go well. He imagined a different conversation. *I missed my flight while on vacation, can you come get me?*

Terry chuckled about it. "No. We can't go there, but Akio probably needs to know what we're up to." Char nodded.

Terry pulled the communication device and activated it. There was no static or buzz, which Terry found disconcerting. He had loved the old Marine Corps radios, which were tough to work with on the best of days. There was nothing like a PRC-77 to ruin your day, the radio which often served as a heavy and unfriendly paperweight.

"Good evening, Terry Henry. How are you today?" Akio asked pleasantly enough. It was eight in the morning by his reckoning.

"What time is it there?" Terry said without thinking.

"Eleven at night."

"Oh crap! I'm sorry, Akio-sama. We've had a few developments here and I wanted to make sure that you knew. I can call back tomorrow morning if you'd like." Terry gritted his teeth. He knew the time difference but hadn't thought about it. He was in his own little world where only he mattered. Char brushed her finger, signaling that he'd been a bad boy.

The nomad was *supreme*, just until he wasn't.

"I prefer the night, actually. It is in my nature, is it not?" Akio asked pleasantly.

"Of course, Akio-sama. We've had a couple additions to our Were family, a Were-tiger and a Were-bear, who oddly enough has taken a liking to the grizzly cub who came with us from New Boulder," Terry started slowly, trying to shape the conversation in a non-threatening way.

"Interesting. Tigers and Bears don't usually join wolf packs. I expect they joined you, Anjin-san, as you continue to steer this boat toward greener shores." Akio's voice was calming for Terry.

Anjin-san, a ship's pilot. Terry knew the word because of reading James Clavell's novel, *Shogun*.

"We've also encountered a Forsaken," Terry added without further explanation.

"How did that encounter end?" Akio asked in a colder, measured voice. He hadn't been satisfied with the explanation-free version of Terry's report.

"We beat the holy crap out of him, and he submitted. He has committed to working for me," Terry added quickly.

"I will warn you, Anjin-san. Forsaken are not to be trusted. They are self-serving. He will turn on you when you least expect it. Be very wary around him. Never turn your back on this Forsaken." There was an edge to Akio's voice that sent a chill down Terry's spine.

"We can arrange something if you'd like to meet him yourself," Terry offered. "He is coming tomorrow morning, our time, and that would be best because he'll get into our minds and know that we've talked. Right now, he doesn't expect you."

"Until then, Anjin-san. I look forward to meeting the new additions to your family." Akio made to sign off.

"Since you mentioned that, Akio-sama, Charumati and I are expecting our first child, a daughter, we believe." Terry looked at Char and smiled.

"My congratulations to you both," Akio said, his pleasant and uplifting voice had returned. "Until tomorrow." There was no click, but Terry felt that the line had gone dead.

"He doesn't like your pet Forsaken," Char taunted Terry.

"I'm losing control, aren't I?" Terry knew the answer she'd give. She knew that he knew, but they still liked to dance.

"You never had control, TH," she said, showing her teeth in a broad smile. Kae let go and ran ahead. They joined hands and walked after him. "Maybe you have this animal magnetism that attracts the creatures of the wild to you. Or maybe, they all believe that we can be a better humanity than we were before, or you'll beat the crap out of them."

Terry was humored.

"You started all this, you and that pack of yours," Terry said mysteriously.

"Oh, really," Char said in her best condescending tone.

"A few years ago, I was on my own in the mountains, hiding from mankind, until a pack of Werewolves chased me off a cliff and into a mountain stream. You wouldn't know anything about that, would you?"

"That might not have been me. Marcus was the one who decided it was fun to hunt humans. Have I mentioned lately how glad I am that he's gone?"

"Not today, but the day is young, my love," Terry told her. "I want my own boat."

"Of course you do, dear. I have two kids, soon to be three, but at least the women won't be outnumbered, not that we ever were," Char replied.

"We better go see the FDG, get them ready for tomorrow and tell the pack, too. We'll tell Ted whenever he gets back with my boat." Terry smiled devilishly as he ran after Kaeden.

CHAPTER NINE

lemson and EssCee were beside themselves. They'd lost five cattle in the dust storm that had blown through. The livestock had gotten out from behind the wind break, then staggered the wrong direction and gotten buried.

The herd was already hard enough to expand and they'd been making progress, up until they left New Boulder.

"Dad's not going to be happy," EssCee told his brother.

"He'll be happy when we make it to our new home with whatever cattle we have left," Clemson said, trying to believe his own argument.

Adams shook the dirt off his clothes as he joined them. "What's the damage?"

"Five of ours, none of the longhorns," Clemson reported. Everett, Hayden and the rest of Eli's grandchildren were trying to brush the red dust from the backs of all the cows in the combined herd.

"We did the best we could." Adams shrugged. He knew the importance of the herd as a food source, especially with the added mass of humanity that he was bringing with him.

"Get them ready to go, we leave as soon as we can find the road." The boys nodded and got back to work, joining the others cleaning off the cows, wiping the crust from their faces.

Adams turned back and saw the young men trying to look manlier as they worked with the cattle. Three of Eli's five grandchildren were girls and the competition was getting fierce.

The nightly chuck-the-rock contests were taking on a life of their own.

It allowed everyone to blow off steam and forget about the trials of the road, if only for a little while.

Adams looked down at his boots, which were about an inch too short to wade through the dust. The red powder cleared the top and wedged itself between the leather and his ankle. He continued to wade through it, cutting a path to the road. Once on it, the way east was clear, but the river ran to the northeast, away from the road.

Water was life. To the east stood an endless red plain without a single speck of green. "When the fires of Hell have passed, all that remains is death," Adams philosophized to himself.

Adams returned to the group, and thanked the chief profusely for the warning that had saved lives. Then he outlined the rest of the day's travel plans, as in, they were going to keep following the Missouri River. There was too much risk heading across the open country, especially with the recent dust storm.

Adams gathered the people and cupped his hands around his mouth so he could better project his voice.

"We're going to add a week at least to our journey, but as long as we have water, we shouldn't lose any more cattle. And I don't want to lose any people, no matter what. An extra week is worth the price," Adams shouted to the large group, hoping to be heard over the noise the cows were making.

The chief suggested they stay an extra day in order to process the cattle that died in the storm. "Mother Earth frowns on those who waste her precious resources," Foxtail added.

"And there you have it! We'll be staying here until we recover all that meat. We know where two of them ended up. Let's spread out and find the other three!" The people shuffled away, FDG, farmers, natives, and the other members of the mob, as Adams had taken to calling it.

Adams pulled the chief aside so he could apologize for not getting his input first. Foxtail appreciated the effort, but confirmed that Adams was in charge of getting the group to their new home and that the chief was simply a passenger on this bus.

"Of course, Chief. Let's butcher a few cows and celebrate life."

"My thoughts, exactly, my friend," the chief said softly.

❖ ❖ ❖

"Form the platoon!" Terry bellowed as he approached the barracks, surprised by the lack of activity. He went inside and saw that it was empty. "Where'd they go?" he asked.

Char used her senses and explored the area, finding her fellow Weres, the farmers who were trying to prepare a field, a group fishing on the shore to the south, some people hunting and the rest inside various buildings. One across from the dining facility that Claire and Margie Rose were running seemed to have a number comparable to what they were expecting.

"I think they moved," Char said.

"Indeed, oh grand master of the obvious. Do you know to where they may have gone?" Terry asked.

"I do," she replied as she strolled away.

Terry followed, feeling even less in control than he usually did.

Akio wasn't going to be pleased with the magnanimously arrogant Terry Henry Walton. He was convinced of that. The line between good and evil had been clear, but Terry had blurred it, like the chalk of a base line in a game that has gone on too long.

If Terry hadn't blurred the lines, Char wouldn't be in his life. Terry decided that he couldn't be the final arbiter of what was good or evil, which confused him since that was exactly what the Force de Guerre was about, to protect the one from the other.

Or was it. He wanted sufficient firepower to force people to talk. His belief was that the good people in the world only needed the opportunity to put it on display. To do that, they had to feel safe.

The FDG was a force for good.

And if Akio kicked his ass for it, so be it. When Terry finished talking with himself, he discovered that Char was a hundred yards ahead with Kae, waiting patiently.

I bet you're in my head right now, aren't you? Terry thought, squinting his eyes as he attempted to mind-meld with his wife. She crossed her arms and twisted her mouth sideways as she looked at him.

Maybe not. He ran to catch up.

It was a short walk to where a number of barracks stood around a compound faced by a dining facility that the Force affectionately called the chow hall.

They ran into Mrs. Grimes as she shuffled her way toward it.

"I seem to have lost my platoon," Terry said with a smile.

She stabbed a thumb over her shoulder toward the building behind her, harumphed, and kept walking.

"I think the boys may have been bad," Char guessed.

Terry made a sharp right turn and headed straight for the building. He heard the shouting well before he opened the door. He held it for Char and Kae. They walked into a nice entryway, with hallways to the right and left. Char headed toward the noise, because she knew that was where TH would want to go.

She was indifferent to it all, but he loved his platoon and the control he wielded over it.

The veins stood out on Mark's neck as he vibrated with fury. Jim and Ivan were arguing over one of the rooms.

"Report!" Terry bellowed down the hallway, making everyone wince from the volume.

Jim and Ivan jumped to attention. Mark's mouth worked but no sound came out.

Char stepped out of the way and he smiled at her, tussling Kaeden's hair before moving past and putting his nose an inch from Mark's cheek.

He whispered, "I think I motherfucking said to report."

"Yes, sir!" Mark was finally able to get out. "We're establishing room assignments in the new barracks. Mrs. Grimes didn't approve of the other one."

"Mrs. Grimes didn't approve of the other one," Terry

started slowly. "Since when does Mrs. Grimes run the show here?"

The sergeant broke the position of attention to look sideways at the colonel. "Since always when it comes to chow and the barracks," he replied. Terry turned back to Char. She waved her fingers at him.

"The major is pretty upset that you didn't clear it with her first," Terry said.

"But we did, sir," the sergeant said, nodding.

Terry closed his eyes and turned back toward Char. She mouthed the words "no control."

Terry took a moment to compose himself. "What's the argument about, Sergeant?"

"Tell him, you fucking morons!" Mark yelled at the two men still standing at attention. The colonel casually turned, not happy that Mark passed the buck.

"I wanted this room," Jim said calmly.

"I wanted it first," Ivan replied.

"And there you have it, the complete text of the last twenty minutes of my life," Mark whined.

"I am Groot, huh?" No one understood the reference. "Neither of you get it. It's mine for when the Mrs. is mad at me since we don't have a couch. Let's see what we have here."

Terry pulled the two men into the hallway and walked into the room. It was a barracks room, with a shared bathroom linking it to the next room over. Too bad the plumbing wasn't operational. There was no furniture.

When Terry returned to the hallway, Jim had Ivan on the ground while Mark laid across Jim's back, trying to get him into a headlock.

"Gentlemen?" he said softly. They continued to grunt and twist. Terry leaned closer. "Gentlemen?"

Jim arched his back trying to throw Mark, but when the back of Mark's head slammed into Terry's chin, he was through.

He drove a right cross into the back of Jim's head, followed with a left roundhouse into the side of Mark's face, then he picked Jim up by the back of his pants and threw him down the hallway. He didn't fly very far before landing in a heap.

Ivan covered his face. Terry kicked him in the leg.

"Get up!" he ordered the three men. The empty hallway was suddenly filled on both sides with the remaining members of the platoon. The three men stood haphazardly after the swift but harsh punishment that had been meted out.

But the punishments weren't finished.

"You! You're busted back to corporal. You take over third squad. You, back to the end of the line. Do you get me, Private?" Terry tipped his chin at Jim. "And you, if I could bust you any lower, I would." Terry snorted like a bull ready to charge, then composed himself to continue.

"Sergeant James, you are now the platoon sergeant and, Corporal Lacy, you're now in charge of first squad. Sergeant, Corporal, congratulations. Get this barracks squared away by evening chow, and then formation tomorrow at dawn, full gear, be ready for individual combat training. It's on the schedule for all day."

Char nodded her approval.

Terry looked at the shocked faces in the hallway, no one was moving, people were barely breathing. As he turned, he brushed close to Mark. "I expect you to work your way back up, do you understand me?"

"Yes, sir!" the man replied, not feeling as confident as he tried to sound.

MARTELLE AND ANDERLE

❖ ❖ ❖

Ted didn't sail very far down the coast. He only wanted to keep the boat out of Terry's hands, but he realized he had too much to do, and Gene could help him bring the Mini Cooper to life. Ted was unsure of the fuel within and if it wasn't fueled, he had an idea where to get some, but once again needed help to get it ready for use.

In either case, having another nuclear engineer on hand was a huge benefit. Even if he was a monstrous brute.

Ted executed a quick turn and sailed back up the coast. He slid the boat into the harbor with a well-practiced hand.

A number of town's people were fishing using various tools and were having reasonably good luck. Fish would probably be a staple for a while. What they needed was a commercial sized fishing trawler, then they wouldn't have to hunt.

His wolves enjoyed fish and he found that it was good for their coats, keeping them nice and soft. He gave the fishermen a thumbs up to encourage them in their efforts as he tied his boat to the dock, furled the sail, and put the cover over it.

Ted walked back to the plant to find Timmons elbow deep in something innocuous.

"We need to talk with Gene," Ted suggested. Timmons wasn't amused.

"No, we don't. If you want to, go right ahead." Timmons shoved his arms back into his project.

"Fine." Ted stomped away with no idea where Gene would be. He decided he'd ask Billy. He opened the door and almost ran into the Were-bear. Hank/Bogdan, standing by the giant's side, started sniffing Ted.

"Nice kitty." Ted reached out to pet the grizzly cub's head, then thought better of it.

"My nuclear physicist best friend!" the man bellowed from two feet away.

"Nuclear engineering, actually," Ted replied, wondering if the big man heard anything he was saying.

"No matter, tiny, we see plant now, okay?" Gene held the door open for Ted to return inside.

Gene and Bogdan both worked their way through the door, before Gene decided the inside of the plant was no place for the grizzly cub. He leaned down to talk with the bear, then pushed the door open as Bogdan went outside.

"Were you speaking Russian to him?" Ted wondered.

"Of course, my small friend. All bears speak Russian!" Ted dodged out of the way as Gene attempted to slap him on the back.

"No. No, they don't," Ted tried to say while staying out of the Were-bear's reach.

CHAPTER TEN

Dude, this is boring as shit," Boris sneered, looking at the ground, then the way ahead, and back at the ground. Adams scrunched his face in frustration.

"Why are you telling me?"

"Because the colonel said you never whine to the troops, that if you have to cry, do it to the next one up the chain, and that's you," Boris explained.

"I can follow that logic. Is this where I'm supposed to placate you with something exciting while agreeing with you heart and soul?" Adams knew how the game was played. He didn't enjoy playing it, but it was turning into a long walk.

A really long walk and he was bored out of his mind, too.

"They say that peace in one's soul comes from peace of mind." Adams peered at Boris through one eye, wondering if he bought it. The look on the young man's face suggested he saw it for what it was.

"That's bullshit, and I know bullshit after stepping in it for the last thousand miles. What? Is that supposed to make me feel less bored? Here I am in the middle of nowhere, bored and being fed bullshit." Boris would have continued if Adams hadn't stopped him.

"It was worth a try," Adams conceded, before biting the inside of his lip. "What do you want to be when you grow up, Boris?"

"I have no idea, Adams. I'm not sure I like this—" Boris swept his hand around him, taking in the cattle and a barren horizon. "—but I do like this." He finished by pointing at his uniform shirt.

"The Force de Guerre. I guess I've been drafted into it as well because of Char. I think it's a good thing, but don't have much experience with Terry and what he expects. I have an idea, but prefer to hear what you have to say. You've been with him from the start, right?" Adams looked intently at the corporal, curious and suddenly hungry for the information.

"I was the second group. He beat the fuck out of me as part of my interview. What do you think of that?" Boris chuckled inwardly, shaking his head and smiling. "I was an arrogant prick, told him that I was the last of the Marines. I didn't know that he had been in the Marines. I have no idea how old he is, but damn, before I knew it, I was flat on my back and choking on my own tongue."

Adams nodded slowly, wondering why the man thought back to that moment with such affection.

Boris continued. "The colonel is about personal honor. Say what you're going to do, then do it in order to build trust. Selfless service. Be the biggest and the baddest, ready to bring down the thunder on anyone who threatens our people, all the while praying to God that we don't have to kill anyone. I know, it seems weird. The colonel said that if we have to use force, we've already failed. And then he goes to war against those Vampires."

Adams's breath caught in his throat and he pinched his lips together. His eyes misted as he was instantly taken back to the mountain. Thank God for Terry Henry Walton and Charumati, otherwise he'd be dead, too. Part of him died in that mountain, but part of him had lived.

His alphas had come to his rescue and delivered the vengeance he wished he could have been there for. It was because he wasn't fast enough, he and Xandrie weren't disciplined enough.

"I guess we all need to learn how to fight better," Adams said softly, his mind still in the mountain where his body was broken and covered in blood.

"Yeah, we have a lot to learn. Maybe instead of playing chuck the rock, we practice, man-to-man combat?" Boris suggested, looking at Adams hopefully.

"One round of chuck the rock, then we break off, maybe bring the oldest Weathers boys, the oldest Eli kid, too, maybe even some of the braves. This is a hard world. There's nothing wrong with being able to defend yourself, make a good showing at least. Isn't that part of personal honor, pride in your own abilities?"

Boris wasn't sure. He needed to think about that. "Pride, not arrogance, as I learned the hard way." Boris pushed Adams playfully. "A smart dude once told me that peace of mind is found in soul food."

❖ ❖ ❖

James stood at the head of the platoon in front of their new barracks. Mark was in the back leading third squad, a sad looking Blackbeard standing next to him. Corporal Lacy was at the front left of the formation as the squad leader in charge of first squad. They were standing at attention as the colonel and major arrived.

A lone civilian stood behind the formation. Terry went to her first.

"What are you doing here, Kiwi?" he asked, coming across as judgmental, which wasn't his intent. The young woman looked hurt as she wondered how to answer.

"I'm sorry, that's not what I meant. It is always good to see you. How is your grandmother?" He placed a gentle hand on her shoulder as he waited patiently for an answer.

She stood tall and proud. "She is well, thank you. Gerry and I will be married on the rest day. We would be honored if you would be there."

"We wouldn't miss that for the world and congratulations again, Horse Master Kiwidinok." Terry took his hand from her shoulder and held it out for her to shake. She gripped it in two hands and smiled.

"Autumn Dawn has asked me to be a part of our native delegation, participate in the meetings to represent our people," she said in a low voice, looking left and right to make sure no one was near, before she added in a conspiratorial tone. "I have no idea what I'd be doing there."

"Report!" Char called from the front of the platoon. Terry felt like he'd missed something and was instantly anxious, ready to run to the front of the formation. Control, Char had said. He didn't need to control every little thing.

"First and third squads all present. Second squad

remains on detached duty somewhere near the Wastelands," James reported boldly.

Char was filling her role as executive officer, being the major that he'd promoted her to. Terry turned back to Kiwi. "Watch what the elders do, understand why they do it, and then you'll see how they can guide you without telling you what to do. Actions mean more than words."

"Gerry and I have been watching you and Char. We want our relationship to be like yours, equal partners, which is a good lesson for my people. I think it would make them better, stronger," Kiwi said, drifting off as she thought about how that would appear to the other members of her tribe.

"Sounds like you already understand what you want to get out of life. It's not a destination, but a journey. You will inspire many others to do what you have done, command your own purpose." Terry looked into her brown eyes, studying her. The rebellious youth from months ago was gone, replaced by a mature young woman deciding on her own path forward.

"Open ranks," James bellowed, "march!" First squad took two steps forward. "Side straddle hops, on my count..."

Char walked casually around the formation.

"Slacking off, Major?" Terry asked, smiling at his beautiful XO.

"I won't dignify that with a response, although you should probably get your weak ass into formation and PT with the rest of them. I'll be along shortly. Since I'm maid of honor in the upcoming wedding, we have some things to talk about." Char made a shooing motion with her hand, while smiling and wrapping the other arm around Kiwi to pull her close for a hug.

"Where am I when you are doing all this stuff, talking

with all the people, knowing everything?" Terry complained. He looked confused.

Char shooed him away a second time, preferring to keep the key to her success secret. She ushered Kiwi farther from the formation. Terry saw Aaron and Kae standing to the side and waved for both of them to join him.

When they arrived, he started doing jumping jacks—what the military called side-straddle hops—in time with the rest of the platoon. Kaeden was no stranger to calisthenics. Aaron was, looking very much like a flamingo as he jumped out of rhythm.

Terry couldn't watch.

A movement coming toward the formation caught his eye. He saw First Sergeant Blevin in a shuffling run with Corporal Heitz and a couple of the other drivers.

Blevin ran up to Terry and saluted. "I'm sorry, sir. I didn't know we had a formation otherwise I would have been here on time. My fault completely. I won't let it happen again. We were coming to get chow before starting work in the motor pool. That's when we realized we were AWOL," the first sergeant said breathlessly as his chest heaved trying to suck in more air.

"Get with Sergeant James after PT and make sure he keeps you informed. We've got individual combat training this morning which could be a little rough. You can watch, but I can't have my A-Team getting hurt!" Terry smiled at them, showing his pleasure that they'd joined the formation. He waved them to take their places at the back of the formation.

"At ease!" he called when the exercise stopped and walked to the front. "You've met First Sergeant Blevin and our good people from the motor pool. They are the Motor Transport

Platoon, with the first sergeant in charge. They will be kept informed of everything we do. They are, as of this moment, active and honored members of the Force de Guerre."

Blevin waved to the platoon. He had no idea what was in store for his first day back on active duty.

❖ ❖ ❖

Gene sniffed the air with his bear snout, using the heightened senses of his Were form to take in his surroundings. Bogdan lay half off the mattress, snorting in his sleep. Gene kicked the cub with his massive paw. The grizzly woke up for a second, then rolled over, snuffling and smacking his bear lips.

Gene stretched, then changed into his human form and got dressed. He looked at the bear cub. "You shed like goat!" he told his new friend. It was the middle of winter, but had yet to get cold. It was far cooler than the Wastelands, but to the grizzly, it was time to shed his winter coat.

The home they'd been given was at the very edge of the base, closest to the overgrown golf course on the southern side. Gene went behind the house to relieve himself. The grizzly cub joined him, sniffing at the puddle that Gene left behind, before following him as the large man headed for the chow hall, where he'd been told he could get his meals.

He noted that a number of the Werewolves and the Weretiger were in the open area in front of the kitchen and dining area, but his fellow nuke wasn't there. Gene saw that Ted was still in his quarters, as was Timmons, the engineer. He shrugged since he didn't really care what all the others were doing, but he also felt something different.

A Forsaken approaching from the big city. He thought about telling Terry Henry Walton, but decided not to bother.

If the Werewolves couldn't sense him, then they deserved what they got.

Gene set out. Breakfast sounded good, something prepared by someone else sounded even better. He couldn't remember the last time he didn't catch or find his own food.

It had been too long.

Bogdan followed happily, sniffing at places where the wolf pack had marked. The pack was in the woods behind the house he'd been given. He watched them in his mind for a moment. Once certain they were keeping their distance, he continued his long strides toward the chow hall.

There was a great deal of noise from the human contingent in the square. Gene stopped and watched, recognizing the military calisthenics. He grimaced thinking back to his time in the Russian Army where the workouts were ridiculous. His real workouts were orders of magnitude better. Getting juiced by the team doctors didn't hurt either and accounted for his massive size. That was before the Kurtherian changes made to his body which turned him into a Were-bear.

And he grew even bigger, to the point of being a monster, assuring him that he wouldn't fit in anywhere. After the WWDE, he'd migrated across the pole and into Canada. It wasn't an easy trip, but he had to leave the nuclear wasteland of Russia.

The trip. His mind drifted back.

The polar bear had surged from the ocean onto the ice flow that Yevgenniy was riding. The ice shifted from the weight of the dripping white beast. In the Arctic, polar bears were at the top of the food chain.

Gene didn't care. As a Were-bear, he was every

bit as big as the great white predator. Gene crouched and roared. The polar bear roared back and ambled forward two quick steps, trying to drive his next meal backwards. Gene held his ground, paws firmly braced on the ice pack.

He waited. The polar bear inched forward. With a powerful lunge, Gene launched himself at the polar bear, driving his front claws into the beast's thick neck. He held tightly to keep the white jaws away from him.

The polar bear rolled backward and brought up his back claws to rake down Gene's stomach, shredding the flesh and tearing into the muscle. The bear's front paws latched onto Gene's front legs and that was when the Were-bear knew that a change of tactics was in order.

He drove with his back legs and once the polar bear was off balance, Gene twisted and forced it to the ice. The floe bobbed dangerously, threatening to dump both fighters into the ocean, a place where Gene didn't want to be.

Gene raked his claws through the white fur, the blubber, and into the neck muscles. He dug deeper and deeper as the polar bear roared in pain. The Arctic cold disappeared as both bears fought for their lives.

In the end, one would feed on the other to survive.

Gene's arms were starting to go numb from the loss of blood; the nanocytes weren't keeping up. He needed to finish the fight and feed. With a surge of power, he twisted the polar bear's head, but even with his great strength, the polar bear's neck was unbreakable.

The great white beast growled and panted from the pressure Gene was putting on its throat. The ice floe tipped and they slid to the edge. He clamped down on *the bear's throat with his remaining strength. Polar bears could hold their breath for an extended period of time, but not in the middle of an epic battle.*

It flailed to throw Gene off, trying to remove the pressure, keeping it from taking a breath. With one last push, Gene drove both of them over the edge and into the freezing water. The Were-bear let up on the other beast's throat, but stayed underwater with it until it gulped water into its lungs, filling them for one last flail before it stilled. Gene started swimming for the surface.

Blood trailed from the horrible wounds on Gene's body, a string of his entrails floated lazily in the water as he fought against the water and his own exhaustion. He dragged the loser to the floe, pulling himself up first, then muscled the polar bear onto the ice after him. Gene stuffed his own guts back in through the wound, which made him retch violently.

He recovered enough to disembowel the polar bear, and Gene stuffed himself, then he snuggled halfway beneath it, using its wet fur for warmth.

He lay there holding the wound on his stomach to help them while they healed, all the while hoping that another predator couldn't smell the blood.

He could only hope that there wasn't one nearby as he passed out.

Gene came back to himself as Bogdan recognized the human called Blackbeard. The grizzly cub ran to meet his friend. Then the child, Kaeden, intercepted the bear and the free-for-all commenced. Blackie broke ranks and Char dismissed the platoon so they could play with the bear cub.

Terry and Char met Gene halfway across the square.

Gene looked at the pair before turning to Terry. "Forsaken come up road from city. Be here in ten minutes."

"Thanks. We were expecting him. It's good to see he's on time. This one owes us for not killing him," Terry replied casually, watching to gauge Gene's reaction. "Do you have a problem with the Forsaken?"

Terry was curious. The answer seemed to always be universally negative.

"Who doesn't have problem with Forsaken?" Gene's voice boomed and echoed. "You have big guns and army. We have no problem with Vampire. Come, we eat now." Gene turned and walked past the scrum that was the bear cub and half the platoon. The older men of Motor T were less inclined toward wrestling and followed Gene toward the dining facility.

Aaron extracted Kaeden from the pile and joined Terry and Char standing to the side.

"Sergeant James! Chow for the next ten minutes," Terry called and watched the platoon break contact and run for the chow hall where Claire, Antioch, Mrs. Grimes, or Margie Rose would be waiting to dish out something from the communal food supply.

CHAPTER
ELEVEN

More food, woman!" Gene bellowed at Mrs. Grimes from the other side of the serving counter. He leaned as far over the top as he could to get closer to the old woman. She stayed put, pulled out her wood spoon, and rapped him on the nose. He stood there in shock so she slapped his nose a second time.

Terry and Char each grabbed a massive arm and yanked the Were-bear backwards.

"He really does need a little more than the rest of us," Terry said, feeling the man's muscles vibrate in anger. "He can have mine."

"And mine," Char offered.

Gene shoved his tray back across the line and Margie Rose slopped two additional servings on top of what was already there. Mashed green something took up half the tray and mystery meat filled the other half.

These were the best meals they were going to get until the farms started producing, and that was months away.

"Here, dear, we can't have you go hungry. This is for the little one!" Margie Rose said with a grin, peeking at Char's mid-section. Char obliged by pulling up her shirt to show her baby bump. The old woman giggled and called Claire from the kitchen.

Kae wondered when he was going to get fed. He held his tray up and nothing was happening. Margie Rose apologized profusely when she saw the little man. He received extra meat, because growing boys and all that. Terry looked hopefully at the two serving trays.

"Move along, mister, there are people waiting." Margie Rose stopped Char when no one was looking and gave her Terry's meal.

The platoon had gone first as they always did, privates eating before corporals eating before the sergeant.

Terry, Char, and Kaeden ate quickly because Joseph was out there on the road, waiting for them. If he got into their minds, he might run before they could stop him.

Then Akio would probably get angry. There was only one person responsible, and he was the one with no control, as he'd been told.

Despite trying to eat quickly, Gene finished in half the time it took Terry, and Terry Henry considered himself a professional speed-eater. He was little league compared to the Were-bear.

No one talked during breakfast, because it was chow time. When Terry wolfed his last bite, he made to stand up, but Char wasn't finished. He took a deep breath and closed his eyes, willing himself to be patient.

"When Ted and Timmons first met the Forsaken,

Timmons ordered James and Lacy and Gerry and Kiwi to think about sex. Ted started making nuclear calculations in his head. The only one who was left vulnerable was Timmons."

Char slowed her eating as Terry stared at her food, wondering why it wasn't getting shoveled into her mouth. She put her fork down and started to laugh at the expression that crossed his face.

"You are transparent, my husband. What if we were going to a ball, or a wedding, wouldn't you want me to take my time and be that much more beautiful when we finally arrive?"

He recognized a trap when he saw one. Since he was already caught, he surrendered. "Of course, dear."

They waited while she ate, but she was only keeping pace with Kaeden. They finished together and took their trays to the scullery where everyone worked doing dishes for the whole town. Margie Rose and Mrs. Grimes chose people as they came through the line for the next day's service. There was no arguing because the alternative was that you wouldn't eat. And while doing the dishes, you were allowed to sample the next meal.

They made it a win-win.

And people got to eat off clean dishes. Each person had carried a plate, bowl, and set of silverware during the journey. When they arrived, it was all consolidated under the watchful eyes of Antioch and Claire.

As Gene was leaving the dining room, he stopped, opened his mouth wide, and belched.

Char punched him in the back, but he wasn't finished with the bass reverberation that some people swore shook the windows. Terry raised his hands over his head and flashed a ten, giving the belch a perfect score. Kaeden laughed and tried to burp, but ended up almost peeing himself.

"Thank God we're having a girl," Char said to herself as she tried to push Gene out of the way, but he was still belching. She wormed her way around him as Kae giggled at the monumental effort of the big man.

The pack was waiting for Char and she called them to her—the Werewolves and the Were-tiger. The Were-bear joined them after finally extricating himself from the chow hall. Char was unsure if Claire would ever allow the man back in without an adult escort.

Even then, probably not.

Char turned to the others—Ted, Timmons, Sue, Shonna, Merrit, and Aaron. "Today we practice our hand-to-hand skills. We train, because not only do we have to be the smartest to help this town, we have to be the fastest. We can't let anyone beat us to the punch, do you get me? So we're going to train with the Forsaken, with Joseph, to get better. And even our large, unmannered friend will join us."

Gene approached, wiping his mouth with one big, hairy arm. He assumed his happy-go-lucky guy persona. "Where is party?" he bellowed, but they knew that he preferred to be alone. Bogdan had been in the square whining because everyone had gone inside. Now that all his friends had returned, he sidled up next to the Were-bear to assume his rightful position. Gene scratched the beast's head.

"Time to go, Gene. Time to meet Joseph," Char stated emotionlessly. Reviewing combat forms and moves, she drilled herself mercilessly until nothing else remained within her mind.

Terry also steeled himself, but he was thinking about sex. He found it was the easiest way to occupy his full mind to complete distraction.

Sergeant James formed the platoon and they marched

behind the colonel and the Were folk. They turned south on the road leading from the base and heading for Joseph, who seemed to be waiting patiently.

When the pack arrived, Terry nodded tersely.

"Today, it's hand-to-hand combat practice, and you're training with us," Char told Joseph through half-closed eyes. Her mind worked diligently through the combat forms.

"Well now. One thinks of combat and the other is obsessed with sex. I see that you two think very much alike, judging from what I see in his mind," Joseph said sarcastically. He seemed to be going out of his way to be disliked by everyone. Gene was the most put out.

He strolled forward and with speed belying his size, he removed his clothes and changed into his Were form. He launched himself at the Forsaken and Joseph was instantly afraid, dodging away. Gene slapped at Joseph as he passed, ripping his shirt with his outstretched claws.

Gene thundered to a stop and turned. Terry rushed to get in between the two. "STOP!" he ordered, but Gene's black eyes were fixated on the Vampire. He charged again.

Terry jumped straight up and twisted in the air. He came down astride Gene's neck and clamped his legs tightly as he wrapped his arms around Gene's head. The Were-bear roared its disapproval of the human rider. He stopped and shook like a dog, trying to throw the human off.

He rolled over backwards and pinned Terry to the ground. Gene wormed back and forth, crushing Terry into the pavement, until the human let go. The Were-bear rolled away. A shadow cast over them, and everyone stopped.

Joseph looked at the descending pod in alarm.

Akio had arrived.

"You bastards!" Joseph yelled, looking for an escape

route. Gene rolled to the side and changed back into human form. He didn't bother to put on his clothes.

Terry stood up and stretched. His ribs popped back into place with an audible snap. "Settle the fuck down, Joseph. Akio is going to check you out. If you told us the truth, you have nothing to worry about. If you lied, well then, that would make you a lying bastard. If that's the case, then you should be worried and better make peace with the creator because your life expectancy can be measured with a stopwatch."

Terry stood next to Char, finding her hand and squeezing it. Char leaned close to his ear. "Your mind control trick is to think about sex?"

Terry grinned sheepishly in response. "If it ain't broke, don't fix it. Joseph had no clue, right?" Char conceded the point.

The back hatch of the pod opened and Akio walked out, hand on the hilt of his ever present katana.

Terry and Char walked forward to meet him.

"Akio-sama, ohayo gozaimasu," Terry said in Japanese— good morning, honored master—and bowed, bending almost ninety degrees at the waist.

"Ohayo gozaimasu, Anjin-san," Akio replied, bending to forty-five degrees, but never taking his eyes from the Forsaken. "And Charumati, good morning, and may I add that you look stunning, glowing even."

Kaeden joined his parents and took Char's hand. Akio kneeled to be closer to eye level with the boy. "Ame futte chi katamaru," Akio said. "Adversity makes one stronger, and in you, I see great strength. I see the power of your adopted parents. Honor will be the wings carrying you on your journey."

Akio put a hand on the boy's head and smiled.

"Can I see your sword?" the boy asked, head held high

and a smile on his face.

"Not today, my son, but someday I will show you." Akio stood and returned to the business at hand.

"His name is Joseph," Char offered. Akio acknowledged that she'd spoken with a tip of his head.

Even with Terry's enhanced vision, he never saw how the sword came to be in Akio's hand or how Akio had covered the distance between the pod and Joseph to hold the blade at the Forsaken's throat.

Joseph didn't move to defend himself, but his lips trembled and he blinked rapidly.

Akio didn't say anything. The Japanese didn't go for the bravado that Terry stooped to on occasion. They considered it to be less than honorable. Akio continued to teach, even when he wasn't teaching.

The two Vampires engaged with each other's mind. Akio was orders of magnitude more powerful than Joseph, in all areas. The Forsaken took his medicine and within his mind, he begged for his life. Akio's sword tapped Joseph's neck and a thin red line appeared. A single drop of blood dripped free, disappearing behind the Vampire's leather collar.

Akio pulled the katana away and slowly sheathed it.

Terry was disappointed because he'd been there when Akio saved him in Syria. He hadn't been close enough to see Akio in action and he wanted that to better visualize what the best looked like. Terry was good, but nothing compared to a true master.

Akio made eye contact with Terry for only a moment, enough to let Terry know that there would be no fighting that day.

Thirty years ago, we would have killed first, asked questions later, Terry thought. *Akio would have killed the Forsaken simply for being what he was, but today is a new day in a new world.*

Gene's lip curled as he looked at Akio. The Were-bear continued to ruffle Bogdan's furry head and round ears. The grizzly cub sat, completely at calm. Only Akio knew why.

Aaron wouldn't look at him until Akio stood in front of the Were-tiger and looked up at the man. There was almost two feet of height difference between them.

"Alone you are strong, together you are stronger," Akio told the man. Aaron pursed his lips and nodded one time, before bowing and almost head-butting the Vampire. He mumbled an apology, but Akio had already moved on.

The Were-bear drew the full attention of the Vampire. Gene was even less transparent with his facial expressions than Joseph. Gene's violent side dominated nearly every aspect of his being. It had saved his life on occasions too numerous to mention. The Vampire made him uncomfortable and put him over the edge. He roared and changed to Were form, shredding his clothes as the Were-bear burst forth.

Bogdan threw himself to the side as the great beast lunged forward, jaws wide to take Akio's head.

But the Vampire wasn't there. No one saw him move, but he was to the side, legs wide as Akio stood in his ready stance. Akio struck, and then returned to his perfect form.

Gene staggered, stumbled, and dropped to his front knees. He shook his great shaggy head, growling as he let the violence within return to the surface. Akio didn't wait. He took one step forward and axe-kicked the Were on the top of his head.

Gene's jaw slapped against the ground first, as the kick drove the bear's head downward. The Were-bear flopped onto its side, breathing slowly as if asleep. Bogdan nuzzled his big friend and laid against him. Akio smiled at the grizzly cub.

He looked at the other Werewolves, one by one. Char was in good graces with the Vampire, and her pack had no choice but to follow her lead. Akio saw that in their minds—they respected their alphas.

Ted's wolf pack was lounging in the grass nearby. Akio sent them a feeling of internal peace. Lids drooped over yellow eyes and soon they were all asleep.

Akio returned to Terry and Char. "Would you please come with me?" he asked. Neither of them thought it was a question. Kae walked with them, but Akio stopped and waved at Aaron. The Were-tiger joined them and took Kae's hand. The boy struggled only for a moment before Aaron lifted him onto his shoulders, where the boy could see so much more of the world. Akio waved to him, and Kae waved back.

A Japanese woman and a shorter girl were waiting in the back of the pod. Without hesitation, Terry walked up the ramp after Akio. Char had flown in the before time, but on commercial jets, just like everyone else. She'd never been on anything like a pod. She stood for a moment at the bottom of the ramp, looked back at the pack and then to Terry. He waved her forward.

"It's okay," he said soothingly.

Once Char was inside, the ramp door closed. They took their seats and the pod lifted smoothly into the air.

CHAPTER TWELVE

Kae waved at the retreating pod.

"I'm sure they'll come home, Kaeden. What do you think we should do today?" Aaron asked casually, still watching the pod as it disappeared into the distance.

The boy scrunched his face up as he tried to decide. "Fishing with Uncle Ted," he finally committed. Aaron looked at Ted. Ted looked at Gene.

Gene didn't look at anyone because he was still unconscious.

"Okay," Ted said and started to walk away. Timmons reached out to stop him.

"Our alpha gave us a plan for today. We practice, individual combat training. That's what we do whether Char is here or not," Timmons explained.

Ted put his hands on his hips. To the untrained eye, he

looked like a fit young man, a hair over six feet tall, but within, Ted wasn't a fighter. He'd taken on the wolf pack alpha out of necessity, but the wolf was grossly overmatched by a Werewolf, even a weaker one. On Ted's worst day, he could still end the fight with a single wolf in seconds.

Against humans, he had no desire to raise a hand. In the new community, he felt safe and swore that he wouldn't fight if he didn't have to. The desire to fight was gone from his psyche. "I politely decline. If I have to make fists, then we've already lost. Aaron, Kae, the boat awaits."

Timmons didn't try to stop him a second time. He couldn't imagine how the giraffe-like man fought. He saved himself the visual by letting the group go.

Joseph's neck had healed, but he kept rubbing the area where the injury had been. Maybe the katana was special. To Timmons, it looked old, probably some samurai's sword from the ancient times. Vampires had a way of collecting the best artifacts, because many of them had lived during those times.

Timmons slowly approached the Forsaken. Sue, Shonna, and Merrit joined him.

"I don't like you, not one bit, but my alpha said that we're to train with you, so that's what we're going to do," Timmons sneered, unhappy with the prospect but knew he'd have to report to Char when she returned.

She wouldn't tolerate anything less than what she asked for.

Joseph looked at the Werewolves and decided not to continue his snark. Terry Henry Walton had accepted him into the fold and the Vampire Akio had let him live, so he must have seen that he didn't have duplicity in his mind. But none of them were here to convince the others.

"What style will you be practicing today? You see that I am a little less practiced in certain forms," Joseph offered.

Timmons started to laugh. "Less practiced? You tried one wimpy-ass kick and ended up face down on the pavement. Dork."

Joseph raised one eyebrow.

"James! What forms are we practicing today?" Timmons asked while still chuckling at the Vampire.

"Marine Corps Martial Arts Green Belt, Gunner, arm bars, choke holds, throws, lower body strikes, and counter-strikes," James called out in a loud voice.

"You lead, Sergeant. Pair people off and let's get to it," Timmons ordered. He wondered if they called him Gunner Fuckface behind his back.

Joseph couldn't control himself. "Gunner Fuckface, now isn't that one to write in the books."

Timmons lost all humor and paired himself with Joseph for the practice sparring.

❖ ❖ ❖

Terry and Char sat silently wondering where they were going or how long they would be gone.

It wasn't more than a couple minutes before Akio and the other two passengers joined them.

"I'd like to introduce Yuko and this is Eve, a product of Yuko's friend, ADAM."

"Pleased to meet you," Char said first, looking kindly at the woman and when she gave Eve her attention, she was surprised to see how the metal flowed seamlessly around the creation's body.

"I am pleased to make your acquaintance, Yuko-san, and

you, too, Eve! We spent so much time talking about door codes, I feel like I know you," Terry quipped.

"Thank you, Terry Henry Walton," Eve started in an almost musical voice. "That effort took only thirty-one percent of the estimated timeframe for a calculated ninety percent chance of success. I was pleased with the result."

Terry nodded. Only one-third as long as it could have taken. He hadn't realized how lucky they'd been. It was all a matter of perspective.

Akio waited until the pleasantries were finished before he started to talk.

"I wanted to show you something before I asked for your help," Akio said in a soft tone with a slight bow to his head.

"I'm not sure how we can say no," Terry replied, watching Akio while holding Char's hand. She squeezed lightly to let him know that she agreed. They didn't feel pressured, but there was no way they could turn Akio down.

"We have future plans for New York City and there's something disturbing ongoing that we need nipped in the bud sooner rather than later," Akio said conversationally. It made the situation seem less extreme, but this was Akio. It was a big deal for him to ask. Terry understood that.

"Please continue, Akio-sama," Terry urged, fighting the desire to put a hand on the man's shoulder as a friendly gesture. He expected that Akio didn't like to be touched.

He had no desire to test his theory.

"An individual has set himself up as a warlord. This by itself wouldn't concern us, but he has surrounded himself with a number of humans, including women and children. We'd like to see those people liberated, if possible, and the warlord disposed of," Akio said. "We need New York City to be reestablished, so killing as few of the humans as possible is important to us. The population needs to grow."

"Is the warlord special in some way?" Char asked. Terry was thinking about the innocents and what he needed to do to make sure that his people treated them as refugees and not enemy combatants.

It was a difficult task and one where hesitation could be deadly. The FDG needed to identify friend or foe at a glance, then act accordingly. Every single member of the platoon needed to get it right. It was a significant undertaking.

"He is a Forsaken, not a daywalker either. I will join you for the sole purpose of removing the Forsaken from power. I need you to do the rest, deal with the humans and save them." Akio sounded like he was pleading.

For the sake of humanity, Terry and Char had to take the job.

❖ ❖ ❖

Ted unfurled the sail and it snapped tight in the brisk breeze. Aaron hung halfway outside the boat to avoid getting hit by the beam as it whipped back and forth with Ted's tacks.

Kae was at home in the boat since he'd been in it before; he had just enough experience to give him an artificial level of confidence. Ted made him sit down so he wouldn't accidentally fall out. "Can you swim, Aaron?" Ted asked.

"Yes, but for some odd reason, I really don't like getting wet and I don't float at all, too skinny, I guess," Aaron answered, looking at himself as if the answer would be there.

"You're a cat. Of course you don't like getting wet," Ted said matter-of-factly. "But you should love fish."

"I do. Speaking of that, when are we going to start fishing? I'm hungry. That big oaf messed with my breakfast."

Ted shook his head. He hadn't gone into the chow hall when he saw that Gene was there. He expected some level of discord any time the Were-bear was around.

Ted had taken the boat south. The base was still in sight. The wind was strong, probably more like the usual wind as opposed to the mild winter winds they'd had that year.

They'd gone not more than two miles when they ran across a larger container vessel that had run ashore, probably right around the WWDE. It was settled into the lake shelf and created a large reef. The growth on the hull drew the fisherman in Ted. He suspected it was home to many different varieties of tasty fish.

"We need to catch at least ten so I can feed my wolves," Ted said, setting the performance standard.

"And leave nothing for us? Twenty, Sir Theodore, or bust!" Aaron said grandiosely, waving one arm over his head, hitting the sail. "Oh, sorry."

"Twenty or bust!" Kaeden called in his small voice.

"Okay, twenty then," Ted conceded, all the while keeping a weather eye on the horizon.

❖ ❖ ❖

Joseph's mouth was bleeding. He ran a dark tongue over his lips to collect the blood before it got away. He smacked his lips and waved Timmons forward.

They were supposed to be working on leg strikes and defenses, but the intensity of their engagement had become an anything-goes sparring session. The rest of the platoon and the pack surrounded the two fighters, who appeared to be equally matched.

Timmons had underestimated Joseph's abilities based

on how easily Terry Henry had beaten the Forsaken. Maybe Timmons overestimated his own abilities, when he should have known better. He lasted less than one second against the colonel. At least Joseph was able to get up on his own after his fight.

Timmons had his hands up and bobbed his head like a boxer. James was disappointed because they weren't using any of the techniques he'd been teaching.

Joseph only had a couple hours of practice in the techniques, but he was employing the blocks and counterstrikes. The Forsaken seemed like a natural.

James wondered why the man fought as one with no experience.

Timmons attacked, feinting with a couple jabs before trying a leg sweep. Joseph easily dodged it and spun, catching Timmons in the middle of his chest with a roundhouse kick. The heel of Joseph's boot hit like a sledgehammer. The Werewolf grunted as he stumbled backward.

But he didn't fall. Joseph danced away, sneering. He was in it to win it. He'd had enough of Timmons' snark and wanted to shove the man's words down his throat.

I have every right to exist as you do, Joseph thought. His eyes glowed red as he worked his way left and right, trying to find an opening. Timmons blocked and parried, connecting again with the side of Joseph's head. The Forsaken blinked the stars away as Timmons laughed.

Blind fury gripped Joseph. He didn't know how he did it, but he moved as the wind—one second here, the next, he had Timmons by the throat and was lifting him and choking him. The Werewolf struggled in his grasp.

Joseph screamed his anger. He turned, carrying Timmons over his head as he slammed the man on the ground behind him. The Forsaken let go, only so he could rear back and put more power into the punch aimed for Timmons' chest. The Werewolf could do nothing to stop it.

The glow from Joseph's eyes was the last thing that Timmons saw as the Vampire's fist drove into his chest, shattering his breast bone and breaking his rib cage. Timmons coughed, splattering blood over his attacker's face.

Joseph wiped it with a finger, then licked the blood off. One of the Force gagged. Ivan had to turn away.

"Enough," James said. The Forsaken's eyes were already dimming. He looked around him at the wary faces. They hated him, and they feared him. Joseph wasn't sure what he wanted from them.

Respect?

He hadn't earned that yet.

He straightened his clothing, adjusted his hat, and turned to leave. "I'll be back in three days, as per my agreement with Colonel Walton."

The bodies separated, creating an opening through which Joseph passed. He started to whistle. It had not been a bad day. The Werewolf's blood was a sweet treat, like M&Ms in the old days.

❖ ❖ ❖

It took a while before they got the first bite, but once they figured out the right depth to fish, they dragged them in each time they dropped their lines in the water. They raced past twenty fish, to thirty, then forty and then they could no longer move as there were too many fish in the well of the boat.

Kaeden was cheering and shouting, despite Ted's urging for silence so he wouldn't chase the fish away. All Aaron wanted to do was get to a place where he could change into his Were form and devour fish to his heart's content.

He dropped his line in expecting a small bite, but something big grabbed the line and nearly jerked it out of his hand. He was already top heavy, leaning far out over the edge of the boat, close to going overboard when he jerked himself back.

The boat rocked dangerously, but Aaron caught himself. Kae wasn't so lucky. He hadn't been prepared for the rocking. He was standing when it happened and was thrown back against the boom, then tossed headfirst overboard. The grounded ship was too close, with sharp steel beneath the water. The shore wasn't that far, but they didn't know if Kae could swim.

Aaron threw his line down, giving up on the great catch, as he crawled under the boom, saw the boy beneath the surface, and he dove in.

He caught the boy in one arm as he slid past, his momentum carrying him toward a mass of jagged steel. He turned to protect the boy with his body. He gasped when he slammed into the knife blades of the shattered hull. Aaron kicked for the surface, tearing his leg open on the way. When he came up, Ted was fighting with the boat to give Aaron space. The sail caught the wind and almost tipped the boat over. Half the fish went back into the water as the sailboat balanced precariously on its side, before righting itself, prow pointed directly at the shore.

The wind filled the sail and drove the boat forward. Ted tried to yank the boom to the side, but it was too late. The keel scraped into the rocks and with a horrible grinding sound. The bottom was ripped from the boat as the rest of it was tossed ashore, taking Ted and a wave of fish with it.

Kaeden sputtered once he hit the surface. His eyes were

wide in panic and he slapped at the water. Aaron tried to calm him as he side-stroked toward the shore. He found the bottom and tried walking, but the rocks were slippery. He stumbled and slid his way ashore, wrenching an ankle and leaving a stream of blood behind them.

Once Kaeden was safely ashore, Aaron shrugged from his clothes and changed into a Were-tiger. He attacked the fish, feeding his ravenous hunger and fueling his nanocytes to repair the damage to his body.

Ted lay on the small beach, looking at his destroyed sailboat. "I guess I can save the sail." He furled the sail and tied it down. He waited until the tiger had his fill, and then Ted stuffed the sail cover with fish and slung it over his back.

"I'm sorry, Kaeden, but we have to walk home," Ted apologized. "Coming?"

Aaron remained in Were form. Kaeden was over his panic, now that he was on dry ground. He picked up Aaron's clothes and walked with them, keeping Ted between him and the lake.

"I don't think I like boating," Kae offered.

Ted remained unperturbed. "Next time, we'll find a bigger boat, a better boat."

CHAPTER THIRTEEN

"If I may ask, Akio-sama, what did you see in Joseph's mind?" Terry asked.

"Even Forsaken deserve their private thoughts, although in most cases, those thoughts die with them as they tend to lose their head around me," Akio offered with a slight smile.

Terry didn't know that Akio made jokes. It seemed unlike him; maybe some of Bethany Anne rubbed off.

"You let him live, Akio-sama. I'll take that to mean we can work with him, keep him close. If he does anything, I will kill Joseph myself, you have my word," Terry promised.

Akio looked into Terry's eyes, then nodded slightly, before looking away. "We are descending, but we won't land. I want you to see what you will be up against."

They peered out the windows as the pod hovered.

"Brooklyn and Queens," Char said. Terry often forgot that

she was from New York City. Her accent had grown milder over the years or he'd gotten used to it. Maybe she didn't have any remnants of the New York accent left. He didn't know.

"What do you see?" Akio asked.

Terry moved behind Char, wrapping an arm around her as he leaned over her to look out her window. She caressed his hand as she focused on the city below. Terry could see the sparkling purple of her eyes reflected in the window. He took a deep breath, smelling her hair, then returned his attention to the terrain where he would conduct a tactical operation.

Mission accomplishment and no one left behind. Those were his two goals. Char would be instrumental in the planning, as well as the others in the pack.

Akio watched Terry Henry Walton and listened to his mind. It was a flurry of activity, but the complete devotion to his wife and intense level of personal honor would have made any samurai proud.

"I see the buildup of an area," Char observed. "A wall, roadblocks even though there are no cars. A fortress of sorts. What used to be a golf course is now a field with crops. People striving to survive, carving a slice from a dead city to become a new city-state."

"I concur. Out of all that, where do you think you would find him?" Akio asked.

"The massive brownstone. It was probably some rich guy's home, with the obligatory Ferrari out front. I never understood the sports cars in a city where if you hit twenty-five miles an hour, you were lucky. You were far more likely to hit a pot hole that would tear up your undercarriage." When Char looked away from the window, she found both men watching her.

Eve seemed to be observing the humans as a whole.

"Okay, I've got some memories that we're not going to revisit. Leave it be!" she insisted, arguing with herself as no one else said anything.

"You would be correct. The brownstone. Can you sense him and the humans?" Akio asked, knowing that she could.

Char closed her eyes and reached out. "Hundreds of humans in that area, dense around the brownstone, but then spreading out. Nearly all of them within the blocked off area."

Terry was instantly frustrated. He wanted the information, the intelligence regarding the enemy in order to plan the best operation, exposing his people to the fewest risks while giving him the greatest chance for success.

"What are our assets, Akio-sama?" Terry asked as he craned his neck to see the area below.

"Your people, whoever you wish, two pods to move them, and your hardware."

Terry's ears perked up. "Is there any way we can pick up some stuff from Cheyenne Mountain?" Terry asked hopefully, like a kid who earned a return trip to the candy store.

◆ ◆ ◆

CHICAGO

Timmons needed help to leave the training area. Shonna was on one side of him and Merrit on the other. He asked them to stop and waved to get James's attention. "Next time, Sergeant, let's train on something a little softer than pavement," Timmons gasped, suffering from the broken ribs that had punctured his lungs.

"I think that's a good call, Gunner. Sorry about that. Next time we'll do better," James replied, wincing as he saw how much pain the man was in.

Shonna and Merrit shuffled away, half-carrying their pack mate.

Gene sat on the ground, leaning against the grizzly cub. Blackbeard joined them. "May I?" he asked. The big man nodded.

"Bogdan likes you," he said thickly, slurring his words, still reeling from the damage that Akio had done to his head. Gene's eyelids were half-closed as he fought to stay conscious.

"We killed his mother," Blackie explained. "She'd eaten one of our horses and charged us. Hank almost got himself shot when he came out of the brush, but we held our fire, and then I couldn't leave the little guy out there."

"It is okay, tiny human. Bears are unpredictable bunch. Just look at me!" Gene chuckled to himself. He had never been beaten, let alone that easily. The Were-bear in him respected strength, making it easy for him to decide to defer to the small man from the pod, the one they called Colonel, his mate, and that angry old woman with the wooden spoon who was serving breakfast.

He'd eaten well, gotten pummeled, was taken care of, and would eat well again.

All in all, not a bad day.

"You visit anytime, tiny human. I like you," Gene said as his eyes rolled back in his head.

"Call me Blackbeard, or Blackie for short," the corporal corrected him.

"Like pirate? That very funny. Blackbeard it is then, my friend. You call me Gene, short for Yevgenniy Stalin, Sergeant in Russian Army, Olympic gold medal winner, and bear." Gene finished speaking and rolled to the side.

"Sergeant!" Blackie called. The platoon was still nursing

their wounds from practicing on the pavement. It wasn't James's finest hour. He hoped the colonel wouldn't be too upset, but James expected to be fired for getting so many people hurt.

"We need to get him back to his home. I'm going to need some help," Blackbeard requested.

James called the platoon over. "Any ideas?"

"I think it's going to take a mess of us to move him," Mark suggested. No one disagreed. Jim moved in first and took an arm, trying to lift Gene. He didn't get very far.

Others joined Jim until there was no more room. With two people under each arm, they hoisted Gene to his feet. He swayed drunkenly. Blackie walked with the grizzly cub as they started the procession toward the base where Gene's home was the closest of all.

They probably wouldn't have made it much further than that.

❖ ❖ ❖

"Why do you remain in so much pain, my friend?" the chief asked. Adams shrugged. Foxtail continued in a soothing voice, "Death and loss are a significant part of life. We celebrate those who have gone before and then we move on. It is our responsibility to live a good life in their absence, never forgetting, but the time for lamentations is past."

Adams didn't think so. Xandrie had been his mate for decades and moving on was one step too far. He had his direction from his alpha, which gave him purpose. He was doing the best he could, and they had only lost five cows, but those five were providing food for the travelers. He'd done well, by anyone's standards, but he didn't get to share the victory with his mate.

He could see her rolling her eyes as he claimed victory, telling him that anyone could have done it, but only to keep him humble. She would have been proud of him as he was proud of what she accomplished.

Maybe he hadn't left her behind, only her physical body.

"Thanks, Chief," Adams said with a smile. Foxtail looked into the Werewolf's yellow eyes. He didn't share what he saw, but he clapped Adams on the shoulder before nodding and walking away.

Boris strolled up. "Where the hell are we? I got a bad feeling about this place."

"Somewhere in the middle of what used to be North Dakota, if I'm not mistaken. Following this river is a bitch. If I only had a map, we could save ourselves a lot of walking since we seem to be back tracking a lot." Adams sighed. The longer the trip took, the more likely they'd start losing people and more cattle.

"We could take a few of the horses and scout ahead, not like we're doing right now with people a half mile out front. I'm thinking ten to twenty miles!" Boris suggested.

"Now that is the best idea I've heard in a long time. Start with two and head out front. Find us the best way ahead, the shortest way where we still have water," Adams ordered.

"Done!" Boris claimed. He ran off to find Charlie and acquire two horses.

"And that is how the Force Cavalry is born and turned loose upon the world," Adams said to himself.

❖ ❖ ❖

The pod crossed the country quickly and landed in front of Cheyenne Mountain, in the area that Terry had cleared with a bulldozer. Akio held Terry and Char back.

"Let Eve go first, she'll move everything you need. Simply point it out."

"There's a tank down there…"

"No," Akio said quickly, winking at Char. Terry sensed a conspiracy, but held his tongue.

"We already moved C4 to Chicago. Flash bangs and non-lethal weapons would probably be handiest." Terry ran through his mind, seeing where everything was stored. The sound of the doors squealing open signaled Eve's success in punching in the code.

"We need to go to the bottom, one of the storerooms. I didn't touch anything non-lethal. There's probably more in there that we can use."

Akio sniffed the air. Terry wrinkled his nose, and Char turned away. The smell of death continued to permeate the place, even though they could hear that the air handling system was running.

"Shall we?" Akio asked as he followed Eve into the dark tunnel.

Terry was about to tell the EI where the light switches were, but she was already there. The lights came on like last time, starting at the top and working their way downhill.

Eve led the way and the other three followed. Yuko had joined them, but she walked more slowly. When Akio saw she was falling behind, he called for Eve to slow down, which she did instantly.

"Eve is an EI?" Terry asked.

"Yes, almost an Artificial Intelligence and honestly, I can't tell the difference. She is our constant companion. I don't know what we would do without her. As a matter of fact, we wouldn't be in here without her." Akio pointed to the tunnel.

"We are doubly blessed by her presence," Char offered.

They continued down the ramp and into the bowels of the mountain. Everything was as they left it. Terry looked for something out of place, unnerved for some reason. He knew the Forsaken were dead, but wondered if anything else had been left behind.

Char assured him there wasn't anything. Akio confirmed that they were alone. The smell of death was being recycled through the system.

"Maybe someday we can burn it all," Terry suggested, "but not yet. Maybe when it's empty."

"Tag what you want and let's go," Char told him. Terry went to work detailing the crates of flash-bang grenades, rubber bullets, and 40mm rounds that packed a net. Which meant he needed the M4 rifles, at least a few with the grenade launcher attached. With a grenade launcher, he'd also tag a couple crates of high explosive 40mm grenades. Maybe white phosphorous, too, in case he needed to start a vicious fire.

"You said this guy wasn't a daywalker?" Terry asked, hesitating and looking up from the crates before him.

"No," Akio replied. "He is powerful but must stay out of the daylight."

Terry stopped what he was doing and tried to imagine how the battle might play out.

"I will address the Forsaken. Your job is to clear the humans out of the way to save their lives." Akio stood still, blinking his dark brown eyes slowly. He rested his hand easily on the hilt of his ever present katana.

"Then that is exactly what we will do, Akio-sama." Terry bowed deeply, then shifted the boxes of non-lethal weaponry that he desired. He went to the armory and removed ten M4 rifles. He slid ten crates of 5.56mm ammunition and a crate of magazines into the passageway for Eve to carry to the pod.

In the garage, Terry looked longingly at the tank. Char pinched his butt when Akio wasn't looking.

Yuko giggled.

There were a few HMMWVs with fifty caliber machine-guns. He left those. If he had to rely on a heavy machine gun, then he'd failed in his mission. He returned to the storeroom and pulled a crate of CS grenades, tear gas. He found masks still sealed, but they weren't any good. He left them. The tear gas would disperse a crowd, and it wouldn't affect him or any of the Werewolves.

Or a Were-bear.

"What kind of havoc do you think Gene would cause?"

"In Queens? Probably as much as you can imagine. You are not thinking about bringing him along, are you?" Char asked pointedly, narrowing her eyes and looking down her nose at him.

"Maybe he and Ted can stay behind and work with the Mini Cooper," Terry suggested. "But we'll need the rest, including Aaron."

"Aaron stays behind to watch Kaeden," Char answered. Her body language suggested that her statement was definitive and not up for discussion. "He can't remember what he does as a Were. That alarms me."

"Me too, lover. I don't know why, but I feel like Kaeden should be with us."

"In the middle of a fight? Are you stoned?" Char put her hands on her hips, glaring at Terry defiantly. "He was in this mountain with us because we had no choice. Now we do. Aaron is a godsend. We need to do a better job of protecting our children, TH!"

"But we're going to Brooklyn, and you're coming, too,

aren't you?" Terry asked, knowing that she was. "Is that your idea of protecting our baby?"

Terry approached his wife and mirrored her pose. Akio and Yuko excused themselves and left the garage.

Char's eyes sparkled under the fluorescent lighting. He thought that she was radiant. Whether from the pregnancy or not, he didn't care. He slipped his hands around her waist and bent to kiss her. Char draped her arms over his shoulders and around his neck, pulling his face to hers.

CHAPTER FOURTEEN

People were fishing along the shore and in the base's small harbor. Kaeden had his hand in the neck fur of the great tiger while Ted walked stoically, not making eye contact with anyone as he didn't want to answer any questions.

But it was inevitable. "Where's your boat?" someone asked. Ted ignored them, but Kaeden didn't. He stopped and the tiger stayed between the boy and the fisherman, eyeing the man warily.

"It broke apart on the rocks, but we saved some of the fish!" Kae replied, upbeat and smiling as long as he wasn't too close to the water.

The man mumbled something and went back to his fishing. Ted walked around the harbor and then headed inland. He started whistling once he cleared the trees. Aaron changed into his human form and Kaeden handed him his clothes. The tall man dressed quickly while they waited.

The wolf pack loped toward them, ten shaggy beasts with tongues lolling. He opened the sail wrap and dispensed the fish. "Don't you forget how to hunt, you lazy bastards!" Ted told them. If they did, he'd keep feeding them, but they needed a good hunt to sharpen their skills.

"I think I'll take you hunting tomorrow. Inland, away from the lake," Ted said, nodding once as if the deal was sealed.

"I want to go!" Kaeden added.

"I don't think so, Kaeden. We will hunt as wolves, moving quickly. In any case, it will be up to Terry and Char," Ted replied.

Kaeden huffed and stomped his feet. He was still a little boy.

Aaron took Kae's hand and the remaining fish from Ted, and started walking toward the chow hall. "I don't know about you, little man, but I am hungry. All that swimming took it out of me," Aaron said, looking at where his clothes were ripped from the sharp edges of the dead ship. His wounds were closed, but his nanocytes demanded more energy to keep healing him.

Kae thought it was a good idea. He was always hungry. If Terry and Char had a measuring stick, they would have seen that the boy had already grown a couple inches since he'd been with them.

That much growing took energy. "Me, too, Aaron. Chow's up!" he called in his little voice, repeating what he'd heard Terry say.

❖ ❖ ❖

Terry and Char each carried two heavy crates as they climbed the ramp back to the pod. They deposited them behind what Eve had already loaded. Yuko offered tea, which Terry and Char graciously accepted. Terry had been a coffee guy, but that died with the rest of the world. He hoped that someday, he would taste again of the black nectar of life.

Yuko produced an insulated pot from which she poured tea into small cups. Terry and Char cradled them in their hands, waiting to see how Akio drank his. Once he took a sip, they followed suit.

When the desired crates had been moved to the pod, the lights inside the mountain were turned off, and the doors secured, Terry wanted to double-check. Akio stopped him.

"No need, Anjin-san. All is as Eve said." Akio motioned that everyone should take their seats. "I think it is time to go. I would like to show you something on our way back to your home."

Neither Terry nor Char asked what it was. They'd find out soon enough.

Akio sat back and closed his eyes. To Terry and Char, he looked like he was asleep. They turned in their seats and peered out the window. It had been a long time since they'd flown. They'd just traveled from Chicago to New York City to the Rockies and were heading back to Chicago. All in half a day, including the time it took to find and load the munitions Terry wanted.

The Wastelands were mostly barren, crisscrossed by streams and windbreaks of trees. The red dirt was pervasive throughout. It looked like a vast desert when only decades previously, it had been called the heartland. Now it was called the Wastelands, the Fallen Lands.

The pod continued north. On the horizon, Terry made

out the green fields on both sides of the Missouri River. The pod started to descend and Akio opened his eyes. Terry and Char saw the mass of humanity and small herd of cattle.

Char could feel Adams and the others, almost two hundred people in total.

The pod rotated as it landed. The hatch opened and they looked out on an open field. Adams was running toward them.

"Stopping by to say hi, see how things are going, then we'll have to be on our way," Terry quipped, smiling and holding out his hand.

Adams saluted as Boris had taught him, then shook Terry's hand. Char smiled back. She could see the calm on his face.

"Thank you," he told her simply. "On a side note, we have company who decided that go west young man was for the birds. They said Mother Earth was going to swallow their village and they decided it was time to see greener pastures. I present to you, every-freaking-body and their cows."

Adams swept a hand to encompass the entirety of the field before them. The chief was obvious since he was wearing his headdress. He walked deliberately toward them, skeptical at first, but when he saw Terry and Char, he brightened considerably.

Akio waited on the ramp. Eve and Yuko were nowhere to be seen.

"Chief Foxtail, isn't this a pleasant surprise. I have to say that I'm quite pleased that you and your people will be joining us. We have plenty of room," Terry suggested.

"I'm happy to hear you say that because we are coming. It would be a depressing walk to think the whole time that there was no place for us," the chief replied.

"You are always welcome by our fire," Char said. The chief hugged her.

"Well then, what is this fine looking piece of technology? I didn't think anything like this survived," the chief wondered, looking at the pod. Akio held up a hand.

"I am sorry, Chief Foxtail, but I am unable to show you the pod at this time. Please do not take it personally. I don't show it to anyone, but I needed their help." Akio nodded toward Terry and Char.

"To wit," Terry began. "With you and your people, we can leave you the rifles, ammunition, and horses, if you'd like, because I could use Boris and his squad. We have a job we need to do and I'd like the platoon intact."

"And me?" Adams wondered, cocking his head. He seemed unsure as to which answer he preferred.

Char looked at him closely, studying him. "I think I'd like you to stay with the chief and all the people. They need you here and it seems that your time on the trail is serving you well."

The chief put a hand on Adams's shoulder and nodded. "It is doing us all some good. My people will scout ahead and keep us on track. We have lost five cows in a dust storm that nearly caught us in the open. Otherwise, we are well."

With that settled, Terry looked for a way to round up his squad. Boris and Charlie were miles ahead. The others were scattered far and wide. "Can you get me a horse, Adams?" Terry asked.

In no time, a horse materialized and Terry made a quick circuit around the group, finding the FDG members and sending them running toward the pod. One of the farmers pointed the way ahead where Boris and Charlie had gone. Terry thanked them and rode back to the pod.

Char gave the chief a crash course in how to use the AK-47 while Terry was rounding up the Force warriors. All of them handed over their rifles and ammunition to those who remained. They were only to be used in case of an emergency and even then, the chief wasn't so sure.

"Would you please send a couple of your people ahead to where Boris and Charlie are scouting? Tell them to wait and if it's okay with Akio, we'll pick them up in the pod." The chief waved one rider to him. He gave the young woman instructions and sent her away.

Akio pulled the chief to the side and the two spoke congenially for a few minutes. Even with Terry's enhanced hearing, he couldn't understand what they were saying. Akio bowed and the chief raised his right hand in respect.

Akio signaled for the others to embark. Terry directed the men to their seats along the inside of the pod. The ramp closed, and the vehicle lifted into the air and smoothly accelerated forward. It couldn't have been more than twenty seconds later when they set down again.

The ramp opened and Terry saw Boris and Charlie watching them intensely. They'd seen the pod before, but they never expected to see the colonel and the major in one, or that they'd be ordering them to leave their horses and rifles and hop aboard.

The chief had no intention of giving out the rifles or ammunition. He intended to put it all in one of the carts and forget about it. He was afraid to think what such weapons would do in the hands of the untrained. There was already a great deal to fear without adding to it.

Terry and Char didn't think that the Force might be terrified of flying. They'd never flown before.

Any of them.

MARTELLE AND ANDERLE

❖ ❖ ❖

CHICAGO

When Sue walked into Billy's office, he wanted to know what was going on.

She was sore from having hit the pavement more than once. Shonna, Merrit, and Sue had practiced together, going through forms and getting back into hand-to-hand combat techniques. It had been a while since they trained like that.

It was gratifying, but in a painful way. Sue worked a sore shoulder as she looked at Billy, Felicity, and Marcie.

Clyde had stayed with Billy that morning and was happy to see Sue finally return.

"Did I hear that the pod arrived? What did Akio want? I can't find Terry and Char anywhere. I need answers!" Billy spewed his words out.

"Akio wanted to assess the one we know as Joseph, a Forsaken. He beat the crap out of Gene, and then he took Terry and Char with him when he flew away. Outside of that, nothing happened," Sue replied.

Billy sputtered. "Terry and Char left? Where'd they go?"

Sue shrugged as she petted Clyde using her good arm.

"But, they didn't tell me anything!"

"Billy's feelings are hurt, if you can't tell," Felicity drawled softly as Marcie crawled around on the floor. Clyde wanted to go outside and run. He'd been cooped up all day.

"No idea where they went. I can tell you they weren't expecting it, but being what Akio is, you don't turn him down when he asks you to do something," Sue explained. "I got the impression they'd be coming back."

Billy grumbled and fussed with a couple papers on his

metal desk. "What's a Forsaken?"

"That is a good question, Billy. Do you remember the old vampire movies?" Billy nodded. He liked scary movies. It was the only thing he'd watch on television. Usually, he had gone out to make trouble.

"They are like the old vampires. They drink human blood for nourishment. They eat people food too, for what it's worth," Sue told him.

"They drink human blood and Walton brought it here?" Billy stood and pounded on his desk. Marcie started to cry. Felicity angrily looked his way.

"Keep your friends close and your enemies closer, right?" Sue quoted. "There's nothing to worry about. We can take him if he gets out of line. Terry has Joseph's word that he won't feed on any of our people."

Sue's words didn't placate Billy, and seeing what an enraged Joseph had done to Timmons, she wasn't so sure the Werewolves could defeat the Forsaken in a battle. It was best that they not find out, but to be sure, they needed Terry Henry Walton and Charumati back.

They were the force behind everything that had been accomplished. Terry and Char were the reason that Joseph was in their control in the first place. Terry had beaten Joseph into submission and made it look easy. Terry had beaten Timmons and made that look even easier.

Sue was certain the whole town needed the alphas, as they were the strength of the pack.

"Come on, Clyde. Let's get some fresh air!" Sue said happily, throwing her blond hair over her shoulder as she tossed her head and walked out.

"Do you have any idea what's going on, Felicity?" the mayor asked.

"When it comes to Terry, Char, and the Werewolves, I don't have the foggiest. But the rest of the town is running fine because of you, Billy dear. Have Pepe and Maria been able to make contact with the farmers up north?" Felicity asked, watching out the door as Sue and Clyde ran across the open field in front of the mayor's building.

"Not that I know of, but that's something we need, along with the cattle," Billy shuffled the papers around on his desk, but he wasn't looking at them.

"This place is so much nicer than New Boulder, cooler, the lake, a breeze, and everything," Billy said softly. "Terry was right about North Chicago. And Ted said we have power whenever we need it. But we don't really need it right now, do we?"

Felicity was noncommittal. If they had it, she'd turn the lights on. Without it, they'd use candles, or be fine without light.

But Billy was thinking logistics. It wasn't sexy, but it was what the mayor was responsible for. He wanted power to the freezers and hopefully, they'd still work after twenty years. With the ability to freeze food, they'd be able to start preparing the town for next year, and then the next, until such time when they never had to worry where their next meal was coming from.

It was what the mayor had committed to doing for them.

CHAPTER FIFTEEN

The pod settled into the middle of the old parade deck. The shadow caught Billy Spires' attention, and when he caught sight of the vehicle, he left Felicity and Marcie behind as he ran outside.

The rear hatch opened and seven members of the Force de Guerre lined out, breathing deeply of the fresh air and looking relieved to be on solid ground.

They made a chain where they passed crates from man to man until there was a large stack on the ground.

Terry Henry Walton and Charumati remained inside until all the crates were out. Terry and Char bowed deeply to a Japanese man who bowed back. Billy assumed that was Akio and wanted to meet him.

He rushed to the pod, but with one word from Terry, Boris stopped him. "You're not allowed on the pod, sir. Please wait here."

Billy was furious and tried to push past, but the Force members were bigger and stronger. They were not going to let Billy inside.

◆ ◆ ◆

"Thank you, Akio-sama. We will see you in three days. At that time, we'll meet you right here with the full platoon and our additional specialists."

"You mean Were folk and the Forsaken," Akio said simply, not attacking Terry. He'd made it clear that he'd leave the tactical planning for the operation in Terry and Char's hands. If they wanted the Forsaken along, that was their business. If the Forsaken got out of hand, then he would become Akio's business.

"I almost forgot, Akio-sama. When we found Kaeden, he mentioned that the girls from the group had been taken. I promised him that we would find them. I don't know where to look, but would move hell and earth to bring them home." Terry bowed deeply.

"Anjin-san always thinking of others. Who am I to say no to such an honorable request? We will do what we can. Until next time, Anjin-san." Akio bowed.

Terry and Char strode from the pod, turned to watch the ramp close, and waved as it silently lifted off and flew away.

"Let me go, you fucking asswipe!" Billy yelled. Felicity was standing behind him and trying to cover Marcie's ears. Terry crooked his head to look at the mayor.

"Billy Spires, great to see you, my man!" Terry called happily, before turning to Boris. "Secure this gear in our armory before you do anything else. And then, assemble the platoon. We've got some work to do."

Boris stood there looking confused. He had no idea where the armory was, the platoon, or even where he was.

Char started to laugh and waved Terry away, even though he'd already turned his attention toward the mayor.

"Billy, I know you're upset," Terry said softly as he guided Billy away from the others. "It's not my place to say whether you get to meet Akio or not. He is a very private man and generally doesn't meet with people. I met him before the fall and it appears that we have a relationship, which means he's comfortable enough to talk with me, but that's it. Please don't take it personally, Billy."

"How can I not take it personally, TH? I'm responsible for all of this and I just got here myself. I'm still trying to figure out a way to feed and clothe these people, let alone deal with the menagerie of creatures that you seem to gather to you. That fucking bear! Holy shit, Terry!"

Clyde appeared and rubbed his dog face on Billy's leg. The mayor scratched his ears without thinking. Terry put his hand down and Clyde sniffed it, wagging his tail furiously. Terry reached inside a shirt pocket and pulled out a meat stick. Clyde wolfed it down and looked at the human, wondering where he was hiding the rest.

"About the bear, he might be a little sore for the next couple days. He pissed Akio off and got his ass beat. When we left, he was still on the ground. I wonder if he's dead?" Terry wasn't concerned either way, which he found disconcerting in its own right. He'd accepted Gene into the fold, but if he'd gotten himself killed, that was his own damn fault.

There was too much for Terry to do to babysit grown adults.

Terry watched Char and Boris head in the direction of the new barracks. They started jogging and soon disappeared around a corner.

"What's this stuff?" Billy asked nodding toward the crates.

"Non-lethal weaponry. We've got a job to do for Akio in New York City. We'll be flying out in three days, taking the platoon and the Char's people," Terry replied.

"That's it, huh, motherfucker?" Billy said getting a little too close to Terry's face. "You're my security chief, and you'll do as I tell you!"

Terry chuckled. "That ship sailed a long time ago, Billy. Don't make me rip off your head and shit down your neck just to make a point. We need each other, but we're on separate paths. You take care of the town and its people, and I will guarantee that you can do it peacefully. It's a partnership, Billy," Terry stated, enunciating clearly and speaking slowly.

"Partners my ass. You work for me, shrivel dick!" Billy's face was turning red. Felicity shook her head, wondering why her husband had fits of rage where he felt it necessary to poke the bear.

Terry wrapped an arm over Billy's small shoulders. The mayor tried to shrug it off, but Terry gripped his shoulder firmly. He turned Billy away from the others and with his free hand, he grabbed Billy's hand, isolating the middle finger and putting pressure on it until the small man thought it was going to break.

"Listen up, Billy Spires, and this is the last time I'm going to say this. Every time you try to assert your authority over me, you end up face down in the mud. Each time you do it, I will have to teach you a lesson and they are going to get more and more painful. Eventually, I'll just have to replace you with her." Terry nodded toward Felicity. "Don't overplay your hand and you won't get the rest of your fingers broken."

Terry tightened his grip and Billy howled as his middle finger was pulled out of its socket. Terry pushed the mayor toward his wife. Felicity sneered at her husband and stormed off. Billy held his hand, looking at the contorted middle finger. He bent over as the pain seized him.

Terry took pity on him. He walked up behind the mayor, grabbed the man's hand, and wrenched the finger back into its socket.

"There you go, Billy Spires, good as new." Terry grinned and slapped the mayor's shoulder. Billy glared at him. "By the way, we just saw Chief Foxtail. He and his people are coming to North Chicago. They're bringing the cattle and the rest of our people, so you might want to put out the word that we've got a couple hundred more people coming."

"I ought to..." He drifted off as he thought better of it. "Partners. Remember that, TH. Don't keep me in the dark, and I'll run a damn fine city."

"That was always the deal, Billy. You've worked wonders for these people, but if you try to control me or the FDG, it won't turn out well for you. So, if you ever want to get laid again, you better go make peace with the missus," Terry encouraged, nodding toward the open doorway leading to the mayor's office.

Billy despised getting shown up, but he set himself up for failure every time. He knew it was wrong to go head to head with Terry Henry Walton, but his ego suffered. He'd always seen himself as King Arthur, but Terry kept showing him what it really meant to be a Knight of the Round Table.

It was Terry's life of sacrifice and pain. Billy slept in his own bed every night. Terry often slept on the ground. Billy knew where his next meal was coming from. Terry often went without.

Billy was angry because Terry was the man he would never be.

MARTELLE AND ANDERLE

Felicity had her arms crossed and tapped one foot while she waited.

She looks really mad, Billy thought, carefully massaging his hand. His finger throbbed, shooting pain up his arm.

❖ ❖ ❖

Aaron took long strides and covered vast distances quickly. Kaeden rode on the tall man's shoulders as often as possible, enjoying the wind blowing past his face.

Kae also refused to let the tall man go since the moment he'd jumped in the water after him and pulled him to the surface so he didn't drown. He carried him to shore, even though the man was hurt.

Yet another person keeping the young man safe. A Were-tiger, a Were-bear, and a Werewolf for a mom. He wondered what fantasy land he'd been dropped into. He hadn't known the other boys in the group all that well. A bunch of families had gotten together and headed south, to get away from the angry men seeking to take over their hometown in Canada. They traveled south. All the parents got sick and died. The survivors continued going, having no idea what they were looking for.

The children were set upon by men on horseback. They killed the oldest boy, a child of fifteen, and took the girls who were younger, maybe seven to twelve years old. The men had kicked the boys to the ground and told them to stay where they were as the kidnappers rode away.

And that was that. The boys continued south until they chanced upon the underground complex, something left over from a different age. There was food inside, but not much. They'd eaten through that and were hungry when they saw Terry ride up.

The older boys thought the kidnappers had returned. They wanted to kill two birds with one stone. Kill the man and eat the horse.

But then the boys kept shooting even after the man yelled out for them to stop, even after the man showed that he would kill them if they kept at it.

Only by chance was Kaeden the one who opened the trap door and then got knocked out by Terry and Char. They told him they carried him to safety while the tunnels caught fire. They hadn't been clear about that, but the older boys had moved the weapons closer to the surface.

Kaeden had been conscious for the explosion. He knew what had happened. Even though they had weapons, the boys found out what it was like to face a far deadlier enemy. When they determined to keep fighting, that was when they lost.

The small boy hadn't known anything about the adults who rescued him. He considered himself lucky. He'd watched them kill with reckless abandon when the situation called for it and then he watched them show mercy. Kaeden puffed out his small chest.

"Don't fuck with my parents!" he yelled, much to Aaron's dismay. He put the boy down.

"Where did that come from, Kaeden?" the tall man asked.

"I was thinking about how Mom and Dad fight. They aren't afraid of anything and boy, do they kick ass!" Kae said proudly.

"I'm not sure they'll be happy with your colorful language. For the record, you didn't get that from me." Aaron hurried toward the central area where Terry and Char had been. He could see the others in the pack descending on them, too.

Even Gene was ambling toward the area.

❖ ❖ ❖

The platoon followed the major, not in formation but as a mob walking and surrounding Boris, bombarding him with questions.

They saw the others and the stacked crates. Terry assumed his best antagonized drill instructor pose and Sergeant James stopped everyone and formed the platoon. He marched them the rest of the way.

Char joined Terry and together they watched the platoon arrive, execute a left face, and then salute the officers. Terry waited for the rest of Boris's squad to join the formation before he returned the salute.

"At ease!" Terry called. There were smiles and there were concerned looks. The platoon was together again, but the rest of the travelers hadn't arrived. They knew something was up.

If they'd been given any time, the platoon would have filled the lack of information with every bit of wild imagination they could fabricate. Terry knew the best way to forestall that was to tell them what he knew.

"We have a mission that only the Force de Guerre can do. In three days' time, two pods will land and we will board them. The whole platoon and some of our specialists will travel to New York City where we will liberate a human population from an evil Forsaken. He has assumed the role of warlord and enslaved a large population," Terry projected his voice for all to hear, including the Were folk who were entering the area.

When Char saw Aaron and Kaeden, she walked toward them. Aaron put the boy down and he ran, yelling, "Mom!"

Terry welcomed the momentary distraction, before turning back to the platoon. "We will form into tactical teams where we'll secure the humans while clearing the way for Akio to enter the home of the warlord and dispatch him. Our job is to minimize human casualties. Period. We will exfiltrate the operation using the pods once Akio has declared the mission objective achieved. We have two full days to train for this mission."

Some of the people shifted uncomfortably. Terry looked closely and noticed the injuries. "What the fuck is wrong with you people?" he demanded.

Sergeant James stepped forward. "Training, sir, my fault. The pavement caused quite a few injuries this morning."

"You're shitting me, right? You did martial arts training on the pavement?" Terry looked shocked. He noticed Timmons walking gingerly.

"And what the fuck is wrong with you?"

"Joseph found his speed and strength. It appears that he can be provoked, and it wasn't pretty," Timmons replied.

Terry closed his eyes and breathed slowly. "Fine. Corporal James, take over third squad. Sergeant Mark, take charge of the platoon and move all this gear to our armory. Secure it and get caught up with your teammates. They have a lot to tell you about life on the road."

James looked both upset and relieved. Mark looked determined, which was exactly what the colonel wanted to see.

Mark marched smartly to the front of the platoon, relieved James, and brought the platoon to attention for one final salute.

"Tomorrow morning, sir, dawn in front of the barracks?" Mark asked. Terry nodded.

Colonel Walton returned the new sergeant's salute, and then gave his full attention to his family.

Char turned Kae loose, who ran to Terry to get picked up. "Ted wrecked his boat and Aaron saved my life!" the boy said excitedly.

"What?" Char exclaimed, looking at Aaron. He explained

the incident, downplaying the danger, but Char knew that Kae couldn't swim and falling overboard was a big issue.

"Ted wrecked the boat?" Terry asked, earning the stink-eye from his wife while he made a show of hugging the little boy.

"We were on our way to the dining facility, if you'd like to join us?" Aaron suggested.

"And you can tell us all about it," Char told the little boy, putting the Were-tiger on alert.

CHAPTER SIXTEEN

Chief Foxtail listened as his scouts reported that the group needed to change direction to the south. The river became a lake and was surrounding them. They'd have to backtrack for miles if they didn't turn now.

The chief issued the order, and the other riders spread the word. The villagers and the cattle would cut across the open as the scouts had directed, and then they'd stop when they hit water in order to fish and refresh.

They were on native lands, a reservation from what Foxtail saw on a sign the previous day. They were walking across Fort Berthold Reservation.

"The scouts reported seeing other natives, too," Foxtail's younger brother Leaping Deer said.

"How many of our fellows are out there?" the chief asked. The younger man shook his head.

I need to meet them, he thought, if for no other reason

than to keep them from making war on the invaders. Foxtail was afraid that people would fall back into the old ways of territoriality and xenophobia. If he couldn't get them to join him, he would leave them in peace and continue taking his people to their new home.

If they would let him leave in peace.

He didn't want to be the chief who uprooted the settlement, only to have them die on the road. He refused to be the chief of a post-fall Wounded Knee. Foxtail didn't want anyone burying his heart, not here, not while he was still young.

The chief hung his head. His younger brother, also a son of Black Feather and Autumn Dawn, had known something was wrong and that their people would travel a dangerous path before settling and becoming one with Mother Earth once again.

"We need to be ready to defend ourselves. We need to be ready to make war," Foxtail intoned sadly.

"Are we not already in a position to make war? We have many braves on horseback. They are watching for any sign of an enemy. Our scouts will keep us from walking into a trap," Leaping Deer recited confidently.

"All of that, yes, but are we ready to kill, brother?" Foxtail stood disquieted, unhappy with the decision that he'd already made. "Bring me our six best, most steady hunters. I will hand out the FDG's rifles and ammunition."

"You've made the right decision, Foxtail," the younger man said, smiling, before he ran off.

The chief's eyes misted and tears threatened to run freely. His younger brother's excitement at carrying a modern weapon was exactly what he feared. He'd never be able to take the weapons back. The genie was out of the bottle, as he'd heard people say.

He had to make the best of a bad situation and then it *came to him*.

He would make it conditional that by accepting the weapons, the men would have to join Terry Henry Walton's FDG once they arrived in Chicago.

Terry would make sure they didn't let the weaponry go to their heads, and the chief could keep the peace in the normal way without having to deal with inflated egos.

He bowed to Mother Earth, thanking her for the idea and the compromise where everyone involved could save face.

And keep the entire group safe.

Peace through superior firepower, they used to say. The chief hoped that was still true.

❖ ❖ ❖

Gene was downright cordial to Mrs. Grimes when he came through the line, even going so far as to apologize for his earlier outburst.

She accepted his apology by giving him a double serving of everything. He sat with Terry, Char, Kae, and Aaron. The rest of Char's pack showed up and joined them.

There was a brief scuffle after Clyde snuck into the chow hall, where Mrs. Grimes and Margie Rose both ended up chasing him, brandishing their wooden spoons, until he decided that being outside was a better idea.

The people eating at the long tables stopped what they were doing and watched, like they would have done in the days of television because good entertainment was always appreciated.

Sue ducked behind Gene so the two gray-haired enforcers wouldn't see her. Timmons and Ted stared at their food, but

Shonna and Merrit wanted to stay in the good graces of those who prepared and served the food.

Merrit yelled, "She's right here!" Shonna pointed.

"Traitors!" Sue said, standing up to take her punishment, which wasn't long in coming.

But she wasn't the target of Margie Rose's ire.

"Terry Henry Walton!" she yelled. Silence was immediate throughout the dining area. The people sensed there would be more entertainment. Terry had just stuffed his mouth full. He pointed at himself with a questioning look, as if his name could be mistaken for anyone else's.

"What did I do?" he mumbled while trying to chew.

"What did you do? You thought it was funny while that creature was stealing my muffins. You encouraged his miscreant behavior. If he ever—" Margie Rose punctuated her points by hitting him in the knuckles with her wooden spoon. "—comes in here again, you will never eat another morsel of our cooking!"

One last knuckle rap for good measure and Margie Rose returned to the serving line, getting high-fived by Mrs. Grimes, who swaggered back into the kitchen.

Char and Kaeden enjoyed watching the beat-down. Sue snickered, happy not to be on the receiving end. Terry gave her his meanest look. She waved him away.

"Very funny. If you get me banned, Sue, I shall be very put out." Terry enunciated each word.

"Forsaken," Char said, dampening everyone's mood.

"We can still take Joseph if we need to," Timmons suggested.

"We have a different Forsaken to deal with and this one is so bad that Akio is going to take care of it himself. That's what he wanted to talk to us about. We're going home, boys and girls, home to New York City where we have to clear a path to a nice brownstone, in which this Forsaken has set himself up as a warlord. We need to do it and kill as few of the humans as we can. We have no idea if any are armed or loyal or slaves. So there you are," Char said, ending by taking a mouthful of something green that looked like seaweed and tasted like cold, wet spinach.

Timmons wasn't sure he'd heard right. "In three days, we're going to go to New York City and fight a bunch of people without killing any of them?"

Terry looked at the ceiling for a moment before speaking. "Sounds about right," he replied and went back to eating, watching Margie Rose as she kept one eye trained on him.

When they made eye contact, she shook her spoon at him. He looked away.

First Sergeant Blevin and Corporal Heitz stopped by the table. "We heard that you're going on an op. Will you be taking any of the vehicles?" Blevin asked.

Terry shook his head.

Blevin looked disappointed. "Can we go?" he asked, hope tinging his voice.

Terry leaned back and looked at the two men, before turning to Char. She nodded almost imperceptibly. He liked the idea, too. Who better to deal with refugees than people who knew what it was like to be at the mercy of a Forsaken?

"Yes, and we could probably use another ten volunteers, because civil affairs are going to play a huge role in this," Terry said, watching them closely. He raised his hand to forestall any premature celebration on their part. "We are going up against a Forsaken, a Vamp like the ones you dealt with. We'll eliminate him, but the people that he's coerced, we have no idea if they are slaves or disciples."

"Fucking A, we want in on that," the first sergeant said determinedly. "Vengeance is mine, sayeth the lord."

Terry hadn't heard any of the survivors quote scripture. He wondered if it was spirituality that kept them alive, or if the first sergeant simply liked the phrase.

"Dawn tomorrow. Have your people out front of the FDG barracks. We've got a lot to talk about and to train for. You ever do any building clearing, like in Iraq or Afghanistan?" Terry asked.

Blevin shook his head, but Heitz nodded and smiled. "You bet, sir. There's nothing like it to get the old heart pumping."

"You got that right," Terry agreed.

"Clear building, no problem. You have grenades?" Gene asked, finally speaking up.

"Since you mention it, yes. We have grenades, both fragmentation and tear gas. We also have a couple thermite in case we need to melt steel or start a really big fire, although I would hesitate before doing that. We don't want to burn down the city. Our job is to save it for humanity. I think Bethany Anne asked Akio to watch over the big cities as they'll be the foundation in our rebuilding, but that's a guess."

"We use grenades," Gene said with some finality.

"Not if it puts humans at risk," Terry countered.

Gene waved a big hand dismissively. "Then we slap them around. They see things our way. Maybe they have vodka and we all be friends?" Gene laughed at his own joke.

The others weren't convinced it would be so easy.

"Sergeant!" Terry called all of a sudden.

He hadn't turned to look, but he knew the non-commissioned officers of the FDG were seated at one table not far away. Mark and James both stood, but James grumbled as he sat back down.

When he reported, Terry didn't bother with pleasantries. "Clear the PT pit of weeds, rake the sand, and find small blocks of wood or whatever to use as buildings. I want to make a sand table, a three-dimensional representation of the terrain, so we can plan this out and get everyone on the same page as to what to expect. Go," Terry ordered, leaning back and staring at a spot on the wall. "I'll be by in an hour and we can get to work."

❖ ❖ ❖

Aaron carried Kaeden so the boy could watch everything that was going on. It had been a long day, highlighted by his near death experience.

The boy didn't let it bother him because he saw the good from it. He'd gotten to eat some of the fish he'd caught as Claire's special treat. His parents had gone and returned. Gene and Timmons were stumbling around because of their injuries from hand-to-hand combat training.

Kaeden looked forward to the time he'd be able to train with his fellow warriors. He didn't have to have special abilities like his parents, because he saw what those in the platoon were capable of. He wanted to learn how to shoot and be the best shot of them all. Even in his small hands, the rifle felt at home.

"Do I get to go?" Kaeden asked.

Char had been waiting for the question. "No, little sweetheart. You and Aaron are going to stay here. Someone has to watch over the town, keep it safe from intruders. Do you have your knife?"

Kae nodded, patting the spot on his shirt where they'd sewn a sheath for him.

"We will be back as soon as humanly possible," Char said, reaching her hand over her head so she could touch her adopted son. "Damn, you're tall."

Terry was on the opposite side, holding her other hand. Her baby bump seemed to be increasing in size hourly. Terry cast furtive glances her way as he didn't want her to see him staring.

He only had months left before the sleepless nights began. A rug muncher, a curtain climber, a chip off the old block. He had no idea if the baby would be born as a Werewolf or be enhanced or be neither.

Terry didn't know how he'd figure it out, although Char said that she would know. He trusted her, but was impatient.

He wanted to know now.

Char yanked on his hand to bring him back to the moment. Kae held out his hands and Terry took him from the Were-tiger, bouncing the boy a couple times before putting him down.

"You know that we're going to need your help when the baby comes," Terry told him.

"What if I don't want to?" Kae offered.

"We're kind of past the options point, little man. All three of us are hanging on for the ride," Terry said, laughing. Char shrugged and smiled, her eyes sparkling wonderfully. "Will your eyes sparkle after the baby's born?"

"Probably more, especially if you make sure that I get plenty of uninterrupted sleep." She grinned.

The trap had been expertly laid and snapped shut on his unsuspecting ass. He tried to think of a witty comeback that didn't make him sound like an inconsiderate prick, but nothing came to mind. He went with his default "safe" phrase.

"Yes, dear."

She mumbled her reply and it wasn't pretty.

Terry shivered, suddenly afraid, as if Margie Rose was chasing him with her spoon.

CHAPTER
SEVENTEEN

Will the pods remain in place after the tactical teams are inserted?" Aaron asked as the four of them walked toward the barracks, expecting the sand to be prepared and ready to be turned into a model where they could best visualize the geography.

"Yes, they will." Terry wondered why he asked.

"Can we go, if we stay with the pod?" Aaron asked, looking at Kae, who nodded.

Terry and Char recognized a conspiracy when they saw one.

Aaron and Kae would abide by Terry and Char's decision, but hadn't thought the previous answer had been definitive and final.

Terry and Char preferred having Kaeden nearby. "If they go, they go on Akio's shuttle and they stay on board, go no farther than the ramp. Aaron is armed." Terry leaned toward them as he spoke. This wasn't up for negotiation.

Aaron held his hands up. "No guns for me. I'd be a significant danger to myself as well as anyone near me." He nodded toward the small boy.

"Fine, but you assume your tiger form and you guard him with your life," Char added.

"As I have already committed to, my lady." Aaron bowed, almost falling as he was still walking. Char shook her head at the tall man, who was so lanky and uncoordinated when in human form, but sleek and graceful as a great cat.

"Then that's what we'll do. Kaeden?" Terry stopped the boy and leaned down to look him in the eye. "You must stay at the pod with Aaron. This is how it has to be. Anything else puts you in great danger. Do you understand me?"

"Yes," the boy said, although he wasn't being fully honest.

"I think we need the king of civil affairs to join us, too, don't you think?" Terry asked Char. "Or should I say, the mayor of civil affairs?"

"You have got to be shitting me. You want to take Billy Spires on a tactical operation?"

"He's had his nose out of joint every time we do something high-speed. It doesn't get any higher speed than this, so yes. In case we need some organizational work for the people, that's Billy's strength. Maybe that will calm him the fuck down, while at the same time show him that we're not playing games. This shit is dangerous."

"I'll set up the sand table." Char rolled her eyes. "You tell Billy and don't be too long about it!"

Terry stood in front of Char and held her face gently in both hands. He kissed her softly while stroking the silver streak of her hair. He no longer noticed how high her body temperature was. The heat was welcome because it was a part of her and had become a part of him.

Their eyes lingered as they walked a few steps away, then Terry turned and headed for the mayor's office.

Char watched him go, thinking she was the lucky one.

❖ ❖ ❖

"What the f—" Billy stopped himself in time. He was still on double-secret probation from Felicity. He had promised at one point to stop swearing around the baby. She was crawling now and any day, she'd be walking and talking. Words might no longer be private.

He smirked.

"You want to go, dipstick?" Terry asked.

"Where?" Billy wondered.

"On the op, to New York City to free a bunch of human slaves, take down a big baddie, you know, the superhero thing, or as we say in the Force de Guerre, business as usual." Terry leaned over the desk and offered Billy his hand.

"No way! So you can break more of my fingers?" Billy leaned back, massaging his middle finger. "Yes. I'll come. That means riding in that funky ship. What'd you call it?"

"A pod. We'll have two of them to carry the entire platoon, our special people, and our new stash of weaponry." Terry smiled. He thought bringing Billy was one of his better ideas.

"Which weapon do I get?" Billy asked.

Terry hadn't thought about that, but wanted something Billy was comfortable with. "The AK-47. We have a lot of those. We liberated a number of carbines from the mountain and half of us will be carrying those. The other half will be carrying the AKs."

Billy pursed his lips as he thought.

"At dawn, the third day from now, the pods will land outside your office. We'll give you your weapon and extra magazines at that time." Terry's tone of voice was directive, not inviting debate. He glanced at Felicity, who stared coldly at Terry Henry. "You'll ride with me. Char will be with Akio. We may need you, so you'll have to stay close to the pod, watch from there, assuming Felicity allows you to go."

Terry fought the desire to laugh, as he'd been stymied in some of his boyish games by his better half. Otherwise, he probably would have had a tank in the motor pool.

Billy hadn't even considered asking her. "Felicity, my darling, my greatest love," he started in his gruff voice. She looked at him sideways and shook her head.

"You can go, but bring me back something nice. I hear New York City shopping used to be the best!" she replied.

"Who'd you hear that from?" Billy asked.

"Duh, Billy! Sue, Char, all of them are from there. Do you think I don't talk with other people?" Felicity said condescendingly. She harumphed, gathered Marcie, and strutted out.

They'd taken a couple of the rooms as their home, so the mayor lived and worked in the same place, just like in New Boulder. He preferred it that way. He missed having the upstairs window, though. He would move upstairs somewhere once they had running water and sewage.

Those who lived in the time before the WWDE would always define modern civilization as not having to use an outhouse.

When utilities were restored, it would be known as the age of revival.

Which reminded him. "When is Ted going to get that

beast off the tracks and start making power?"

"That is a good question, Billy, and the answer is probably after the op some time. Between Ted and Gene, I think they can get it up and running. The big problem is the boiler and piping. As Timmons said, you need power to make power. They've got a dedicated line running from the small plant out back to the big plant up the coast. With the juice and the help of a few power tools, it'll cut a big chunk off the time they need to get it back into service. It'll still be a while, Billy, but Ted will get it done, have no doubt," Terry said confidently.

After a long pause where Billy rubbed the stubble on his chin, he simply said, "Okay."

Terry nodded once and walked out.

❖ ❖ ❖

Char had used the bits and pieces of detritus piled next to the sandpit to build a rough facsimile of the brownstone building and the surrounding area. She studied it intensely while they were hovering over it, enough that she had the details of what she could see. She also filled in spaces with what she could sense and that was how she was able to label buildings as places to sleep and places to work.

She marked the spots where she thought the pods should land, locations that bracketed the brownstone. All movements after that would be to box in the Forsaken, a powerful creature that couldn't tolerate the daylight.

Gene had never been to New York City, but of course he had an opinion. "I do not like big cities. No room for big man like me. Too many assholes."

Ted, Timmons, Shonna, Merrit, Sue, and Char studied the area. Char described where it was and they all said they'd been there, although it had been a while. They talked about one of the best delis on the planet that wasn't far from the brownstone.

The sergeant and corporals watched attentively while Gene kept a hand on Bogdan to keep him from jumping into the freshly cleaned pit. Outside each of the barracks buildings had been a sandpit where the recruits could perform their physical training without putting excess stress on their joints.

Mark and James stood side by side, nodding knowingly. This was where the martial arts training should have taken place and would in the future.

Colonel Terry Henry Walton joined the group and with the help of the native New Yorkers, started to talk through how he thought the operation would unfold. Char filled in the details with the number of humans and where they had been.

Terry had worked before with limited intelligence, but in this case, he could not define the enemy. The humans may or may not fight back, which was the greatest unknown he'd ever faced before going into battle. They might not fire a shot, or they might expend all the ammunition they had. He needed to train the platoon for the widest range of contingencies.

"Think about this, ladies and gentlemen," Terry said, looking at the group of faces, young to old, human to Were. They had a wide range of experience and personalities. Not all of them got along, but Terry didn't care about that.

"We have two days to learn how to execute this operation, minimize human casualties, and achieve the objective," Terry continued to stare down his people. There was nothing more serious at the moment. Even Bogdan and

Clyde were behaving. "We need to learn how to work in an urban environment. We need to practice using non-lethal weapons. And we have two days in which to learn it. Think about it, people. How do we keep the humans out of our fight with the Forsaken? That's it for right now. Be here tomorrow at dawn for PT, then we train."

Ted raised his hand sheepishly. "Including me?"

Terry knew that Ted preferred not to participate in the fighting. There was nothing for him to do if he wasn't going forward. They already had Billy, Aaron, and Kae as observers. Terry didn't want any more non-combatants attached to his team. "Who is going to keep that wolf pack of yours under control if you go with us, Ted? No, you don't need to be here. I expect that you'll be working as hard as we will, just on something else, like my new boat."

Ted was confused as Terry laughed. Kiwi raised a hand, brandishing the sword she'd taken from the crazy that had tried to kill her. She kept her one sleeve rolled up to show off the scar she'd earned in that battle.

"You didn't need to be here, Kiwi," Terry said as she shouldered her way through the others to stand next to the sandpit.

"I want to go and fight," she told them. Terry took a deep breath as the others watched him, ready for him to tell her no.

"Of course you can come," Char interjected as Terry was opening his mouth. He snapped his jaws closed. "We'll need you to protect Billy and the second pod. Aaron and Kae will stay with the first one while it is on the ground. We can't have any of the potential hostiles board the pods while they are waiting for us to return."

Terry mulled it over. Her reasoning made sense. If there

were two of them, it was less likely that Billy would get himself into trouble.

"Have you been practicing with that thing?" Terry asked.

"Every day," Kiwi answered. The muscles in her arms had thickened and toned over the time she'd been away from her village. Gerry worked his way in next to her.

"We're supposed to get married in two days, the afternoon before the op," Gerry said softly.

"There is no better time to celebrate life than before a battle. The wedding will go as planned and we'll all be there," Terry told her, smiling, before turning to Mark. "Sergeant, make sure everyone gets their beauty rest tonight. They're going to need it."

CHAPTER EIGHTEEN

The two days disappeared in a flurry of activity. People were in constant motion. As part of the urban warfare training, doors were kicked in all over the base—a notion that Billy was none too pleased with. They asked a number of the civilians to participate in crowd control exercises.

If it wasn't one thing, it was another. They worked like fiends, running from one training scenario to the next. Terry and Char were exhausted at the end of each day as they were getting less than four hours of sleep. From planning, to training, to executing, Terry wanted to leave nothing to chance.

Gene wanted to take Bogdan. Sue wanted to take Clyde. Terry said no on both accounts. Char argued with him and they compromised.

Both animals were going.

Rapids escorted Autumn Dawn as they watched Kiwi

participate in the exercises, mostly in defense of the mock pod. Billy showed up on occasion, but was put out at having to stand around and do nothing.

He said that he wanted to shoot something. Terry told him that if he shot something, Terry would shoot him.

Kiwi joined some of the crowd control exercises, but she didn't get the non-lethal net-throwing slugs, frag grenades, or rubber bullets. She was awarded the responsibility of carrying a gas grenade in case they were swarmed by people.

Billy was given one too, and he was voted most likely to accidentally discharge it inside the pod because he kept playing with the pin. It looked like he had no friends as the others avoided him.

In order to make the group comfortable with the effects of CS gas, Terry had gathered them close and popped a grenade upwind to let the gas wash over them. There was a significant amount of wailing and running noses. Despite Terry telling them not to touch their face, some people rubbed their eyes. That was the worst thing they could have done.

Terry found that his enhancements made him immune to the effects of the tear gas, something he had wondered about. The Were folk were immune, too, and that was something TH had been counting on. Gene seemed to like it, but Bogdan and Clyde bolted as if lightning struck and thunder crashed.

Sue ran after Clyde, but he was setting a personal speed record in the opposite direction.

The training schedule was impacted as people had to clean up after getting gassed.

The unfortunate part of the CS training was when the wind shifted and took the cloud past the chow hall. Once Claire found out what happened, Terry was banned. He laughed, but she was deadly serious.

So Terry did what he always did when he was put out: he complained to Char.

She had avoided the whole thing as she didn't want to get gassed while pregnant, although they were both certain it would have no effect on the baby.

Terry, being the man that he was, suggested Char remain behind with Kae and Aaron, but she put her foot down and insisted that if Terry was going in, so was she.

He would have been able to argue better if he hadn't been so damn hungry. He wondered when they'd rescind his life-time ban from eating. His nanocytes couldn't save him if they didn't have any energy.

◈ ◈ ◈

Autumn Dawn sat on a chair that Winter Rain had brought for her. She was at the entry to the mayor's building and everything was set up. Rapids had worked with Antioch to sort out the details. Kiwi whipped in on occasion to throw out an idea she had, and then she'd run off again, back to training.

Rapids decided that Kiwi would be too tired to realize that anything had or hadn't been done, so he moved forward with the planning. It was going to be a simple ceremony, but the entire town would be there, which meant standing room only. They put a few chairs up front for the older people and that was it. There was no stage. Antioch wasn't too keen on that since the one in New Boulder collapsed.

When the time came, neither Gerry nor Kiwi were there, nor were any of the others. Autumn Dawn sat calmly, rocking slowly and mumbling prayers to Mother Earth for her granddaughter.

The first person they saw was Char as she strolled into the mostly filled field in front of the large brick building where the mayor made his home. She didn't seem to be in a hurry as she approached. Claire, Margie Rose, and Mrs. Grimes seemed to be the most put out, but no one would yell at a pregnant woman.

Maybe that was why Terry had asked Char to talk with the crowd.

She waved at people as she passed and continued to the front where she talked softly with Kiwi's grandmother first.

"They are in the middle of something and it took a little longer than expected. I expect they'll be here shortly, Autumn Dawn," Char told the old woman as she kneeled in front of her and held both her hands. The elder nodded appreciatively.

Char stood and shouted to the rest of the crowd, informing them that the happy couple would be along momentarily. She walked around and made small talk, hoping that Terry wouldn't keep the platoon for too long.

Everyone stopped when they heard Terry bellow the call to attention. The platoon ran in formation, followed closely by all the others who were participating in the training. Aaron and Gene stood out behind the platoon since they were a head taller than most people.

The townsfolk leaned this way and that, craning their necks to get a better view, but no one could see Kiwi or Gerry.

Terry slowed the platoon and they marched forward, coming to a halt as one. They stood at attention as Terry called out once more.

From one side, Kiwi rode in on her horse and from the other, Gerry rode in on his. The crowd cheered as the couple met in front of the platoon. They stayed in the saddle as they walked forward, through the parting crowd and up front to where Antioch waited for them.

"Good thing we didn't build a platform," he said quietly to himself and got shushed by his wife.

And that was how the wedding went. Kiwidinok and Geronimo got married while sitting on their horses.

◆ ◆ ◆

FORT BERTHOLD RESERVATION, NORTH DAKOTA

Chief Foxtail spent more time getting around the massive lake that dominated the landscape than he was comfortable with. He'd had a bad feeling since they entered the area.

The third day after they passed the sign indicating they were entering a reservation, he realized that he'd been right.

Riders approached from the east. He counted forty or fifty headed his way.

The chief brought his people more tightly together so he could put the men with rifles between them and the riders. He moved up front as the Weathers boys and Eli's grandchildren tried to control the herd, keep them from wandering.

Foxtail personally checked each rifle, making sure the selector lever was set to semi-automatic and that each man held a tight grip. It pained him to see his people that way.

The approaching braves separated into two groups, one went left and the other went right, which stymied Foxtail's attempts to meet them head on.

"We only want to talk!" the chief yelled as the first brave approached. The man on horseback flicked his teeth with a finger and growled as he rode past. Those behind him wore equally grim expressions. They all carried spears. Many thrust them into the air.

"Let them get close, aim as we taught you, and pull the trigger. Ignore the noise and pick your next target," the chief encouraged his men. "Fire when ready."

The first shot rang out almost immediately. A brave that was only twenty feet away was thrown from his horse. The others with rifles hesitated at the sound of the report, but quickly recovered because the incoming riders kicked their horses into a gallop.

They weren't intimidated by the firepower. The first salvo knocked two more from their horses, then three, then five. The horses were past and rode wide.

One of the chief's people, an older man, was speared when he put himself between the riders with spears and a group of children.

"To the sides. Spread out!" Foxtail ordered. Leaping Deer stayed near the chief to defend him. Foxtail carried a knife and nothing else. He hadn't thought he needed to be armed.

More shots rang out as his people ran, shooting at closer targets. The riders were thrown into disarray and rode to a distant point, before rallying, turning, and attacking as a single group. Two of the men with rifles changed their weapons to automatic and cut loose when the riders were only fifty yards away.

They held the triggers down and their magazines quickly emptied. But the attackers' will had been broken. Horses and men alike were on the ground, injured and dying. The chief was torn. He wanted to get his people out of the area, but compassion was the cornerstone of his philosophy. He stood on a small rise and yelled.

"My people! We must help the injured, comfort the dying,

and send the dead on their final journey. Set up camp as we mourn a battle that didn't have to be fought, men who didn't need to die." *And thunder that I didn't want to call down*, he added to himself.

Foxtail grabbed his brother. "Keep the men on alert and guard us while we do what we have to do."

❖ ❖ ❖

NORTH CHICAGO

At dawn of the third day, two pods approached soundlessly from the northwest. They settled into the open area in front of the mayor's building. Timmons watched them descend below the rooftops.

Timmons was waiting for Joseph. He didn't understand why he was dispatched to pick up the Forsaken, but he didn't argue because the alpha had directed him, and she didn't appear to welcome any discussion about it.

He sensed Joseph before he saw him. The Forsaken didn't appear to be in a hurry. Timmons waited as patiently as he could, but then snapped. "Would you pick up the pace, fuckhead?" he yelled.

"What's your hurry, Gunner McFuckface?" Joseph replied.

"We have an appointment in New York City, it seems," Timmons said, curling his lip as he looked at the pasty skin in the shadows of the wide-brimmed hat.

"Why yes, we do have a ride for a quick hop to the Big Apple! Let's see what we have going on, shall we?" Joseph took a quick trip through Timmons's undisciplined mind, seeing the strategy of the attack and the training that they'd been doing the past two days. "Are you sure they want me along, to deal with humans who probably don't have the highest opinion of my kind?"

"Terry Henry Walton said you're coming, so that's the end of it. Now let's go!" Timmons didn't wait as he stalked away. He tried to walk fast, but Joseph sidled up next to him and matched him stride for stride. Timmons was annoyed. He felt that Joseph was mocking him.

"What?" Timmons demanded, stopping.

"Now who's holding us up?" Joseph asked, throwing his hands out as if asking if Timmons wanted a piece of that. Joseph turned and started running. Timmons bolted after him, not wanting to be last to the pods.

Joseph easily maintained his lead no matter how hard Timmons sprinted to catch up.

The two raced into the field where the pods sat. Joseph slowed to better appreciate the view. Terry stepped around one of the pods and waved Joseph to him. The Forsaken assumed his leisurely gait. Timmons jogged past, but Terry signaled for him, too.

Akio, Yuko, and Eve stood on the ramp of one pod while Terry moved to the other. The platoon was split evenly. Char, Aaron, and Kae were on board the first pod with Akio while Shonna, Merrit, Sue, and Gene were with Billy and Kiwi on the other.

Terry put First Sergeant Blevin and Corporal Heitz in the second pod. The other volunteers from the motor pool were balanced between the two vehicles.

Bogdan and Clyde were on the same pod and started to cause trouble so Terry moved Sue to the first pod. Terry looked at Timmons and Joseph, studying them for a moment.

"You, in there." Terry pointed at Timmons and the second

pod. "You with me." Terry walked up the ramp to join Char and Akio in the first pod. Yuko and Eve disappeared up front as soon as Joseph stepped onto the ramp. Akio remained firmly in place.

"In your seats. We leave ASAP!" Terry yelled as he directed traffic, making everyone sit down and buckle up.

Akio took a seat up front and watched as the Force quickly settled in.

When the ramp closed, Terry took his seat next to Char and gave the thumbs up. Without anyone doing anything else, the pod rose swiftly into the air and headed east. The pod climbed for half the flight and then descended.

Terry stared at the floor and rocked himself as he always did on the insert. He visualized the landing zone, ran through the options in his head based on which scenario unfolded the second the ramp came down and his people stormed off. Terry reached to his chest and felt his communication device. He'd call Akio when the way was clear.

Terry watched the second pod take a different angle toward the target as they each headed for their own landing site.

The pod gently touched down. Terry slapped his flak jacket and helmet, shouting "OORAH!" The platoon responded. When the ramp dropped, all hell broke loose.

CHAPTER NINETEEN

Someone had a weapon and they were shooting into the pod. Terry grunted when a round impacted his chest. He turned and stood tall to block Kaeden. "Get him in the back!" Terry ordered and there was a mad scramble as Aaron swept the boy up and held him close.

Kae looked afraid, as he should have been.

The others were running down the ramp and out the back to take up firing positions behind the nearest cover. Terry aimed his M4 carbine out the front and aimed as he headed down the ramp. A round zipped past him and he heard Char gasp as it hit her.

Terry fired rapidly into the window where the shots came from. He hesitated and looked back. Blood streamed down Char's arm, but it had only made her angry. She was already healing. The others were on their feet. Clyde ran past and was barking madly.

He could hear gunfire from the direction of the other pod.

In combat, he who hesitates is lost. Terry yanked his focus back to the matter at hand.

Terry directed the platoon's fire at three different windows as he ran at the door beside them. Suppressing fire tore through the windows and chewed up the bricks around the frame.

Char was right behind Terry and Sue followed. Terry pulled a gas grenade from his harness and dumped it through the window.

He signaled to his riflemen to cease fire.

When he heard people inside coughing, he kicked the door at the knob and bent it, but it didn't break. He called up everything he had for a second try, exploding the door and the wooden barrier behind it. He stepped through then jumped to the side, so he wouldn't be highlighted in the doorway.

Three people. All armed. He waded through the CS smoke and butt-stroked each, knocking them stupid so he could take their weapons. He dragged them outside one by one.

"Tie them up!" he called. A couple oldsters from the motor pool stalked forward and got creative in wrapping the arms and legs of the defenders.

Terry waved the others to him. Char reached out with her senses. "Six more upstairs, I think non-combatants."

"You heard the major! Get up there and clear this building. You are looking for six. Drag them out here to join the others. You two!" Terry called to the old drivers. "Set up a containment area over there. We'll move our detainees to you. Your job is to keep them out of our way; keep them from getting back into the fight."

The two men nodded as they dragged their first three prisoners away.

❖ ❖ ❖

Mark stood at the ramp as it lowered, ready to head out. The first rounds disintegrated when they hit the hull of the pod and bullet shrapnel sprayed over Mark, cutting his face and arms. He yelled, old Marine Corps style, and thumbed his AK off safe. He fired where he saw the muzzle flushes.

"Get the fuck out there!" he yelled and the Force de Guerre rushed past him, staying clear of his line of fire as he covered them. Two men set up at the bottom of the ramp and added to Mark's fire.

The sergeant stopped shooting when he ran out of the pod and joined his people. But he was inexperienced and stood in the open as he surveyed the battleground.

Incoming fire impacted around him. He dodged and ran to the nearest cover, cursing his mistake. He looked about, wondering if it was just his group that had gotten hit. His answer was hearing the rifle fire from the direction of the other pod. Single shots that sounded different from what he was used to, then the fire from an AK-47, joined by the higher pitched 5.56mm rounds fired by the M4.

Billy stood wide-eyed in the pod. Kiwi had pressed herself against the hull as bullets ricocheted off the ground outside. The Force de Guerre, both young members and the oldsters with the neck scars, were systematically laying down fire, like a trained military. They'd run into the fire without hesitation and were doing their jobs.

A roar announced to the world that Gene had changed

into a Were-bear. He rumbled off the pod, drawing all fire to himself. Bogdan followed at a reasonable distance. No one seemed to notice the smaller bear with Gene making all the noise and running directly for the door of the building where the shooting was coming from.

The Force stopped firing as they watched Gene pound past, the ground shaking with his steps. Those in the building hadn't stopped firing and they were shooting at Gene.

"Fire!" Mark yelled, hoping to cover Gene for whatever the Were-bear had in mind.

The Werewolves ran from the pod and took cover. Timmons joined Mark. "There aren't many people in this building, but in the next one over, there's a shitload," Timmons informed him.

Mark thought for a moment. "We clear this one and use it as a base to secure the next building over. The third one is where the Forsaken is," Mark said, thinking out loud.

"We'll just wait. Gene will clear this building by himself. You probably need to have your people ready when the enemy comes running out, terrified." Timmons smiled and watched by peeking out from behind an old, rusted car.

❖ ❖ ❖

Sue stared at the next building over.

"What do you see?" Terry asked as he listened to the firefight around the corner. It was interrupted by a Were-bear's roar, the sound of a door splintering, and then the firing stopped, followed by more roaring as Gene let the world know that he'd conquered his enemies.

"People moving to the windows. Get down!" Sue pulled Terry to the side and he used his body to shield Char as all three of them tumbled to the ground. They crawled to the other side of a stairway into the building before them.

"Do they have guns?" Terry asked.

Sue shrugged. "Maybe?"

"Fuck them," Terry snarled. He jacked a 40mm CS grenade into the launcher attached to his rifle, leaned around the corner, aimed over the top of his barrel, and pulled the trigger. The grenade foomped from the barrel and lobbed through the window.

Terry opened the launcher and dumped the empty, replacing it with another gas grenade. He wasn't ready to start blowing things up. He checked Char's wound. The bullet had grazed her arm and impacted her flak jacket. The tear in the skin was closed and if it weren't for the torn shirt, he would have never known she'd been shot.

With some shouting, six unkempt men and women were shoved bodily down the steps. Terry pointed where they were supposed to go, but the detainees snarled and snapped like wild animals.

He grabbed one woman by her hair and twisted. The bite marks on her neck were there, but only one set. Terry showed Char and Sue. They weren't sure what to think. If they'd been fed on, why were these people acting like they were defending the Alamo?

Terry flung the woman from him. The Force moved them to the containment area where five oldsters were now running the show. They felt sympathetic, but only so far. One of them showed the newcomers his scars and that seemed to calm them. Then the other oldsters pulled their collars down.

The group of detainees became very quiet.

"Time to go," Terry said, putting his war face back on. He

growled as he pointed where he wanted his men to take up their positions.

❖ ❖ ❖

On cue, three of the enemy ran out the front door as they tried to get away from the rampaging bears inside.

"Put down your weapons!" Mark yelled, but that only encouraged them to shoot at him while they ran. The Force opened up, and all three died in a hail of bullets.

Mark modified his orders. "If they come out of the building armed, light 'em up."

"Nope. That place is clear," Timmons told the sergeant. "Now how do you want to go after this next building?"

Mark thought how the Weres were making it easy. They were doing the heavy lifting of assault and gathering intelligence. At least Timmons was letting the sergeant act like he was in charge.

"Tear gas. We'll smoke them out." Mark listened. There was intermittent fire from where the first tactical team was moving closer from the other side, isolating the building with the Forsaken.

Mark loaded a gas grenade into his launcher. The others with the M4s followed suit. The sergeant fired first, taking his best guess on the aim.

His best guess wasn't very good.

The grenade hit five feet below the second story window, bounced off the brick, and fell on the ground where it created a gas barrier between the building and the street.

"Aim high!" he yelled. The second man to fire sent his grenade over the top of the building. The other three adjusted and fired. One grenade out of five went through a window.

Tear gas was massing in front of the building, obscuring the lower windows and crawling slowly toward the sergeant and his people.

"Put a grenade through each of the windows there, sharpshooter," Mark ordered and handed his last 40mm CS grenade to Lacy. She systematically fired the remainder of their stock through five of the six windows. By then, it was time to move, unless they wanted to get run over by the approaching gas cloud.

Mark took three handheld CS grenades and gave them to Timmons. "If you'd be so kind as to pop these through the bottom windows, I would greatly appreciate it."

Timmons took the grenades. "Good call, the people are massing on the first floor. This should chase them out the back door."

"Wait." Mark held out a hand. "Where will they go once they clear out the back?"

Gene roared and ran from the building he'd cleared. Bogdan was close on his tail. He was heading for the building shrouded in CS, but stopped, because Bogdan slid to a stop, then ran back toward the pod.

"What will they do when they go out the back? Who knows…" Timmons replied and ran for the building, pulling the first pin with his teeth.

❖ ❖ ❖

"How many?" Terry asked without turning around. Char and Sue conferred.

"Twenty-two," they finally said. "And we think they have weapons."

"How in the fuck did they get such firepower?" Terry

grumbled as he stood up and made himself a target. His ability to heal allowed him to take risks that he wouldn't let his people take.

"Listen up! I will give you to the count of ten to come out of that building or we will burn the place down," Terry bellowed. Even someone half-deaf would have heard him. "Ten!"

The CS poured out of the downstairs windows. Terry could hear people coughing and hacking. He felt a morbid pleasure in listening to their suffering. Somebody took a shot at him from one of the upper windows. The round bounced off the street two feet to his side. He pointed to the window where the shot came from.

"Light 'em up," he said in a low voice. The mix of AK-47s and M4s barked a deadly staccato. No more shots came from the now destroyed window.

"Nine!" Terry yelled. Someone fired at him from a different window. "Zero!"

Terry stood in the open, changing out the gas round for a high-explosive grenade as his people fired into the windows of the building. He aimed and launched the grenade through a second story window. The explosion threw glass and debris into the street.

Terry reloaded with a second grenade that he sent into the third story window. He looked at Char. "Maybe ten left," she told him.

Joseph stood calmly by her side, making no move to help.

"Clear that building!" he ordered, waving his hand forward. He swung wide and kept his rifle trained on the windows. Boris led his squad up the stairs and into the building. There was yelling and the first of the former inhabitants stumbled out, followed by a grim-faced Force private.

"What are these fuckers thinking, Joseph?"

"They believe the Vampire is their god and when he feeds on them, they become one with him, but not that many have been fed on. We will have no problem with the others, I think," Joseph replied.

Shots were fired inside, then more. Terry couldn't contain himself. He ran up the stairs, throwing the civilians out of the way in order to get in. He climbed to the second floor where the shots had come from.

The area was trashed from the force of Terry's grenade, but many had survived. They'd set up an ambush and Boris had walked into it, but he had taken them out. Charlie was by his side, holding his hand.

Terry swept the area quickly to make sure there wouldn't be any more surprises before joining Boris on the floor. Terry motioned for the others to finish clearing the third floor.

"Kinda walked into it, sir," Boris managed to say, blood bubbling out of his mouth as he talked. One of the enemy had used armor-piercing bullets and they'd gone right through Boris's flak jacket.

"You'll be all right, son, just hold on," Terry tried to console the man, but they both knew it wasn't true.

"I'm sorry," Boris stammered as his eyes fluttered.

"You would have been welcome in my Marine Corps any day, Boris. You were as good as any Marine I ever served with," he told the corporal.

Boris exhaled one last time and that was it. Terry picked him up and carried him to the landing as his warriors roughly pushed three people down the stairs. They staggered and stumbled, still shell-shocked from the grenade that had been tossed their way.

Charlie stopped and without saying a word, held out his

arms so that he could help carry his friend. Terry shook his head as he repositioned Boris over his shoulder.

"I need you in the fight. We have a little more work to do before we get the fucker responsible for this. Are you with me, Corporal?" Terry asked, as he promoted Charlie to take over the squad.

Charlie saluted and took the stairs three at a time as he followed the others into the street.

Terry looked back at the ruin of the building.

"Fucking Forsaken, you started this, but I'm going to finish it," Terry told the body he carried. "Everything we do matters. This matters, maybe not today, Boris, but in a century? Yeah. What we're doing here will shape the future and in a good way. We have to believe that, otherwise the sacrifices are too great."

Terry set his jaw and walked down the steps.

CHAPTER TWENTY

Timmons tossed the gas grenades in and waited. He used the gas cover to strip and change into Were form. He howled with all he had and was joined by Gene's window-shaking roar. The people started to pour out the back. Some opened the front door where Gene ran them over without hesitating. He ripped into the crowd of people, slashing and biting, driving them away in a blind panic.

Timmons ran into the Were-bear and snapped at him, before ducking away. Mark ran into the building behind them, his shirt pulled tightly over his face, but his eyes were watering almost too much to see.

Gene stood on his back legs and tore a fixture from the ceiling as he railed at not being able to wreak havoc on the mass of humanity fleeing before him. Timmons snapped his jaws at the final few to encourage them to quicken their pace.

They ran over their fellows in the rush out the back door.

Timmons changed back into human form so he could block the exit, so the people couldn't return. Mark tried to help but was wracked by a coughing fit when he inhaled too much of the tear gas.

Gene used his massive body to move half a room's worth of furniture against the door. Mark decided that it would hold long enough as he staggered toward the front of the building where he found Shonna and Merrit waiting, standing in a cloud of gas as if it were nothing.

And to them, it wasn't.

Mark envied them as he stumbled down the front steps and across the street to the ruined buildings there where he put his hands on his knees and coughed until he puked.

❖ ❖ ❖

Terry walked from the building carrying Boris's body. He continued to the detainment area and gently laid the man on the ground. The oldsters stood. A couple placed hands over their hearts while the others saluted.

The detainees looked away. They didn't care as they'd seen many of their friends die that day. One of them turned back and stood up, his hands tied behind his back. "Fuck you! Fuck all you!" the man yelled.

Terry was in no mood to be F-bombed.

He stalked up to the man and grabbed him by the collar. The man spit in Terry's face. At the speed of thought, Terry lifted the man using one arm and body-slammed him to the ground, but only hard enough to cause the man a little pain and agony.

"Listen here, cockwad. You fucking assholes fired at us before the door even opened. If you would have waited and talked, we could have avoided all of this. You started this fight by shooting first. So no, fuck you, because there's twenty of your buddies lying dead in their own blood and the rest are out here, tied up and whining like a bunch of hungry puppies."

Terry looked closely at the single bite on the man's neck. "Bitten once and loyal for life? You know it doesn't turn out well for lowly humans, just ask these guys. And one last thing," Terry said as he pursed his lips and made to spit on the man. But his honor prevented him. "Don't spit on me or my people again. I will untie you, and then I will beat you to death with my bare hands."

Terry stood and moved away, but stopped to rest his hand for a moment on Boris's still form, then stalked off, his face set. The mission was coming to its apex.

He gathered the Force de Guerre, the Werewolves, and Joseph for one final brief.

"Blocking positions, there, there, and in the basement of this place." Terry pointed to corners of the brownstone and across the street. He stabbed a finger at the lower windows of the small building next door, the one where Boris had died. "In case he has a tunnel or some other escape route. I want Sue in the back alley. James, take half a squad and give them cover. The rest of the squad, you're in the basement. You others out front with Char and me."

Each group ran crouched to find their positions and prepare for the final battle.

❖ ❖ ❖

Terry crossed the street, hugging the ruins that faced the brownstone. The houses facing the brownstone seemed like they'd been systematically destroyed, so no one could oppose the Forsaken and his lackeys.

Terry saw Mark coming up the street toward him. The man zigzagged as he ran, while Terry stood still. Char joined him and Terry took a position between her and the brownstone.

"No one in the windows, but there are people in there, the basement and upstairs. The basement is two levels deep, by the way. Our buddy has dug himself quite the hole."

Joseph strolled up, hands clasped behind his back as if he were taking a stroll on a sunny day. It was bright with a crystal blue sky, but cool in Queens. No one else had noticed as they'd been too busy, but Joseph had taken it in. He decided that he preferred the weather in Chicago.

"Sir, buildings to the left of the target have been secured," Mark reported breathlessly. His eyes were red and puffy, and his face swollen from too much exposure to the tear gas.

Char suppressed a chuckle. "How in the hell…" Terry asked.

"You made the grenade launcher look easy, sir. I'm sorry to admit that we gassed ourselves." Mark blinked rapidly, hoping his tears would wash away the aptly named agent.

"Kiwi and Billy? Any casualties?" Terry asked.

"None, no injuries. I caught a little bullet shrapnel, but I'm fine," Mark said as his nose ran uncontrollably.

"Bring your detainees to the area over there and deliver them," Terry ordered.

Mark shook his head. "We don't have any. They didn't want to come willingly and Gene was more than happy to oblige them."

Terry felt the pain as it stabbed him right in the heart. If he had adopted that same approach, then Boris would still be alive. *Fuck it all to hell*, he thought.

"Then go get me Timmons and his bunch." Terry slapped the man on the back, then looked at his hand as it was splattered with blood and tear gas. Mark jogged away, staggering as he blinked in the hopes that he'd soon be able to see clearly again.

Gene ambled down the roadway in his Were-bear form with the grizzly cub following closely. Bogdan had rejoined Gene once he had left the tear gas-filled area.

Terry whistled. Surprise was no longer an issue. Gene rumbled toward them. The sight was probably unnerving for anyone other than Terry Henry Walton and his partner Charumati.

Timmons was still buttoning his shirt when he jogged into view with Shonna and Merrit on his tail.

Timmons was first to speak. "He's moving." Char nodded.

Terry pulled the communication device from his pocket. Before Terry could speak, Akio said, "Thank you."

He signed off before Terry could finish his thought.

Akio looked like he was walking slowly, but he flowed past and was into the brownstone before they could blink. Joseph followed him. "Not you," Terry said, but Joseph didn't stop.

"Motherfucker," Terry yelled and came out of the blocks at a full sprint, tackling Joseph as he was about to climb the steps. Terry drilled the Forsaken in the side of the head with a powerful right cross. Joseph's had slammed into the step. The Vampire blinked to get his focus back.

"My apologies, Terry Henry Walton. I didn't mean to ignore you, but I was attempting to look into the mind of my brother down below," Joseph said as he relaxed.

Terry let him up, but only to look him in the eye. "He's your brother?"

"In spirit only. My fraternal brothers are all gone, I believe. This one here is very dangerous, but Akio is not to be trifled with. I would love to watch the fight," Joseph requested.

"I think we would be in the way, so let's stay right here, shall we?" Terry said and leaned against the concrete wall at the side of the stairway. He looked away for an instant to wave Timmons to him.

Joseph appeared to be ready to go inside. Terry stepped forward and grabbed his arm firmly. "If you try to go in there, I will kill you. I promised Akio that I would clear the way for him to deal with the creature below. And that's exactly what I'm going to do."

Joseph's pale skin looked ashen in the sunlight. He shifted uncomfortably to better block the sun with the wide brim of his hat.

"As you wish, Anjin-san," Joseph said sarcastically.

From Akio, it was a compliment. From Joseph, it made him furious. "Gene!" Terry yelled toward the Were-bear. "This thing needs to die."

Terry jumped two steps down and pulled Joseph off balance. With a twist and a heave, Terry threw Joseph over his head. The Vamp landed at the bottom of the steps. Gene lumbered forward and with the unnatural speed of the Were, he pounced.

Joseph dodged the incoming freight train of a Were-bear and rolled to the side, jumping to his feet. He vaulted to the top of the concrete rail and ran the few steps until he could drop to the steps and hide behind Terry. He crouched and held onto Terry's shoulders.

Gene slobbered as he climbed the steps and tried to reach

a huge paw past Terry Henry.

"Call him off!" Joseph cried.

"Why would I want to do that?" Terry replied.

"I wasn't going to help the other one, for piss sake. I told you that I'll work for you, and that hasn't changed," Joseph said while dodging back and forth to keep Terry between him and the Were-bear.

"Gene! Stand down. We'll let him live a little while longer," Terry said, trying to sooth the monster before him.

Gene leaned close and roared in Terry's face. He took it like a man, even though Were-bear breath left much to be desired.

He could have done without the spittle, too.

"Dude!" Terry exclaimed when Gene was finished. The grizzly cub growled from the bottom of the steps.

Joseph closed his eyes and spoke softly, "Akio has found him."

❖ ❖ ❖

Akio slipped the katana free. It sang as only the aged metal could, delicate tones, twinkling as if flowers danced across a piano's keys.

He slashed it through the air, comforted by how it was a natural extension of his arm, almost acting of its own accord.

The Forsaken had a blade, too. Silvered, as if it was made to fight others from the Unknown World. "You've come to do the nasty yourself," he taunted.

Akio didn't reply. That wasn't his way. He darted in, slashing and stabbing to test the Forsaken's style.

He responded, blocking each attack, but it had taken an

effort. Akio was only moving at half-speed in the darkness of the Forsaken's lair.

A lone candle flickered in the corner of the large room. Akio thought it was the workout room, which fit. He would abide by its intended purpose, while being wary of potential traps.

The easiest way to avoid a trap was to quickly dispatch the enemy.

Akio moved at blinding speed and ducked to slash at the Forsaken's legs, but the creature had moved out of the way, almost as if he anticipated Akio's attack.

Not to be dissuaded, Akio feinted one way on a second leg attack and then slashed viciously upward. The Forsaken blocked most of Akio's strike, but the blade tip sheered through the creature's upper thigh, clipping the bone as it passed.

Akio smelled the blood and followed his first strike with a vicious flurry of attacks. The blades seemed to intertwine as they rang a metallic drumbeat. Too fast to follow, the Forsaken was forced backwards. He dragged his leg, willing it to heal more quickly so he could maneuver.

Akio didn't stop. He flowed left and right as if he was a mist blown before a breeze. He swung his katana in arcs around himself at such a speed, it looked like a wall of solid steel.

The sword kept swinging, a soft tone hummed, and the Forsaken felt fear. He was backed against a wall with nothing to protect himself beside his own sword. And it did not sing, but he thought it was time to try.

He started the whirl in front of him and as the blade picked up speed on its first pass, Akio's blade licked in behind it. The sword flew from the Forsaken's hand and clanged from the wall, bouncing harmlessly across the room. The Forsaken grabbed his neck, to stop the blood from spurting.

His heart beat only one more time. With Akio's mighty slash, the Vampire lost his hands and his head, all the parts falling to the floor together. The body toppled slowly, landing with a wet thud.

Akio carefully wiped his blade clean on the dead body's clothes and then put it away. He reached into the etheric and found nothing to threaten him or the others. Even Joseph was under control. Akio walked up the stairs and out the front door, stopping by Terry and Joseph.

"We can leave any time you are ready, Colonel Walton. We have the females to rescue, do we not?"

Terry let go of Joseph. "You know where they are?" Terry asked, smiling, before thrusting his arm in the air and whirling it in a circle.

Time to saddle up.

"Akio-sama, you have done me a great personal favor by finding those who were taken and allowing me to keep my promise to a small boy." Terry bowed deeply. Gene sniffed at Akio's shoes.

They probably had the Forsaken's blood on them. Clyde barked from somewhere nearby and Bogdan ran toward the sound. Rifles fired at a steady pace.

"If you'll excuse me, Akio-sama, I'll be along shortly." Terry tipped his head and ran toward the sound of gunfire. Char yelled at the others to get back to their pods as she dashed after Terry. He was headed down the narrow patch between the brownstone and the building next to it. Situated in the back alley were Sue, James, and half his squad.

Those who'd been chased out by the CS gas were returning and this time, they carried clubs, rocks, and any other weapon they could get their hands on. When Terry and Char squeezed through to get into a position where they could see what was going on, they knew they would run out of ammunition before the mob ran out of people.

"Retrograde!" Terry ordered as he and Char took up firing positions. They popped their last CS grenades and tossed them into the path of the approaching mass of humanity.

James directed his squad down the narrow path, then followed them from the fight. Sue went next, then Char, but not before firing both pistols until the slides locked back on empty chambers. Terry fired judiciously at those who covered their faces and bull-rushed through the tear gas.

Char worked her way between the buildings and Terry did it backwards, which held him up. But once he shot the first person who stuck their face into the crack, it held them back. He had a hard time squeezing his shoulders between the buildings and settled for working his way sideways while watching toward the alley.

Once into the open, he breathed a sigh of relief and ordered the others to their pods. He pulled the pin on one of his precious fragmentation grenades and let the spoon fly as he tossed the device into the space between the buildings. He ran before it blew and collapsed the walls, blocking the space.

He yelled at the oldsters guarding the detainees. They weren't sure what to do with those who were tied up.

"Leave them. Their friends will be along shortly." Terry picked Boris up and carefully draped him over his shoulder. When he boarded the pod, the most important task he had was to account for everyone who should be there.

Clyde nuzzled his hand, just like the old days. Terry called everyone by name then gave a thumbs up to Akio.

The ramp closed as Aaron sat next to Char with Kaeden.

The little boy climbed into her lap and hugged her.

The pod departed and through the window, Terry could see the second pod also lifting off. Into the sky they went, turning west as they gained altitude.

CHAPTER TWENTY-ONE

Terry maneuvered his way across the pod until he was able to kneel in front of Akio.

"The girls, Akio-sama. What do we need to do to help them?" Terry asked, pleading.

"We found a compound in northern Minnesota. It has an unnatural ratio of women to men and appears to be in the style of an old prisoner of war camp."

Terry clenched his jaw and his lip curled of its own accord. He wanted to kill somebody. He looked back at Boris lying on the floor of the pod. Some of the others stared at the body as if they'd never seen death before.

"Just tell us what we need to do, please." Terry pronounced each word carefully and slowly. He was angry at another injustice in the world, but he was getting his chance to fix it.

"We will land outside the range of their weapons and then you will have a free approach to the facility. They have two guard towers which are manned intermittently. Eve was unable to determine a pattern. There will be a total of eight to ten men who are running the compound. They may or may not all be there when we arrive," Akio said softly.

Terry leaned back on his heels and imagined the compound, two guard towers. "Fences? How many girls? Where might the men be?" Terry asked the series of questions, his eyes still closed as he built the image in his mind.

"Barbed wire, gulag style. Twenty-five girls and women. The men could be anywhere, but I expect you will know them when you see them, Anjin-san." Akio kept a straight face, but Terry wondered: had he made a joke?

"Indeed, Akio-sama. Both pods will land side by side?" Akio nodded. "When we land, I will have a plan."

Terry returned to his seat and the pod started its descent. Less than ten minutes to come up with a plan of attack.

The first thing he did, which was what the best tactical planners did, was to take inventory of his supplies. He looked at the crates of weaponry in the middle of the pod. He thought what they'd find on the other pod, then he reviewed the objective.

He couldn't risk the lives of the women, so no fragmentation grenades or HE rounds for the grenade launcher. Net grenades and weapons tight. Don't fire unless fired upon.

The Weres would once again be his shock team. He fingered his M4, wishing he had a different weapon, like a real sniper rifle that he could use to pick off the enemy, one by one.

But he didn't have one of those. He didn't remember seeing one inside Cheyenne Mountain, but there had to be. Someday he'd make another trip back there and find an M40 or maybe even a fifty caliber sniper rifle.

Until then, he had two minutes. He'd have to tell everyone the plan. He closed his eyes and thought through what he wanted to say.

❖ ❖ ❖

The pods touched down and when the back ramps opened, Mark and the group on his ship were confused. It wasn't Chicago. They were in a field of dark green that looked like winter wheat. It was the early afternoon, judging by the sun, and it wasn't oppressively hot, although it was hotter than New York.

They had no idea where they were.

Terry strolled down the ramp of the second pod and waved everyone to him. The menagerie of the group was hard for Terry to fathom. All of them would run into the gunfire if he so ordered.

Except Billy Spires. He saw the small man standing on the ramp, so he could see over the others.

Kiwi was in the middle of the group, holding her husband's hand. James and Lacy had also found each other. Kaeden was riding on Aaron's shoulders. Gene stood to the side with Bogdan between him and Blackbeard. Sue threw a stick for Clyde to chase.

All was right with the world and in a few minutes, things would be right with those inside the compound.

"When we found Kae, he told us that men had taken the girls from his group. We believe those girls are in there." Terry tipped his chin toward the compound where two men had assumed positions within the towers. Terry could see that they carried long rifles.

He motioned for Aaron to put Kae down behind him.

"We're going to go in there and free the girls and the women. The men? They surrender or they die." Terry looked at the grim faces of the group that had just gone through a tough battle, and Terry was asking them to do it all over again.

"This is why the Force de Guerre exists, ladies and gentlemen: to protect the people who can't protect themselves. Our cause is just. We will not harm any of the women, no matter what. We will die ourselves before we harm those we've sworn to protect. Do you understand me?" Terry yelled.

A chorus of oorahs and shouts followed. That wasn't what Terry had been looking for. He only wanted them to know that they weren't to harm the women.

"First squad, left flank, net grenades in your launchers. Third squad, same gear on the right flank. Second squad bringing up the rear. Gene? Are you and Bogdan ready to tear down a fence?"

"Sure, we tear fence, but Bogdan no good at being shot," Gene replied in his heavy Russian accent.

"We'll take care of the men on the tower before we get close. Char? Can you bring me a couple AT-4s, please?"

Char raised one eyebrow, but disappeared into the pod, returning a few moments later with two anti-tank weapons.

Terry tried to take both of them, but Char kept one for herself and signaled that she was ready to go. "Stay safe, Kae. Watch for our signal and when we've cleared things up, we'll wave you in so you can make sure that we've found the girls that you know."

The young boy nodded hopefully. Aaron put a protective hand on the boy's shoulder.

"Billy, Kiwi?" Terry asked. Billy lifted his rifle and made a walking sign with his two fingers. Terry nodded and Kiwi started walking with Billy.

"As soon as we take care of the men in the towers—until then, you two are civilians and need to stay here!" Terry barked and pointed at the ground. Billy held up his rifle as if he was okay to go to war. "No flak jackets. Everyone else has them, so no, you stay here. This won't take too long."

Terry walked boldly into the field and headed past the others as he led the group forward. He waved at first and third squads to move farther away, give them more space. He signaled an inverted V and they assumed that formation without missing a beat. The squad behind him assumed that formation as well. Terry, the Weres, and the Forsaken walked up the middle as a loose group. Terry and Char carried the rockets.

The men in the towers seemed torn. Terry wondered if they'd make it easy. He stopped when he was one hundred yards away, well within the effective range of the weapons the men carried.

He pulled the safety pin near the rear of his AT-4 and flicked the sights up. Char mirrored his movements, then checked the back blast area, moving her pack out of the way.

Once the AT-4 was ready to fire, Terry cupped a hand around his mouth and yelled. "Hello! We are here to free the girls. Please send them out or I'm afraid that we'll have to kill you and then free them. In either case, they'll be freed. Your only choice is whether you want to live or die."

Char looked at her husband. "What the hell was that?"

"They made me mad. You know I can't be trusted with diplomacy when I'm angry," Terry explained, keeping his eyes on the men in towers.

"Then let me do it next time," she argued. He nodded.

"Blow the tower on the right?" he asked pleasantly.

"Sounds good." Char checked her back blast area again and once sure it was clear, she aimed and let the unguided rocket fly. It wooshed from the barrel, sending a long flame from the back of the launcher. Shonna, Sue, and Merrit ran to the area to stomp out the small grass fires that had started.

Joseph stood to the side and chuckled to himself.

The rocket flew true and hit the cupola at the top of the tower dead on. It exploded in a shower of fire. The man in the second tower slid down the ladder and ran for one of the buildings. Terry used his weapon to blow the main gate. Terry and Char threw the spent casings aside and pulled their weapons as they walked—Terry, the M4 and Char, her two Glock pistols.

Terry rested one hand on his whip, comforted by its feel on his hip. He turned back and saw Akio, Yuko, and Eve standing next to Aaron and Kaeden.

"I think we have five men in that building to the left and the rest are mixed in with the women," Char told him.

On cue, shots rang out from the building to the left.

"Damn, fresh out of rockets," Terry quipped, then turned to first squad. "Kill everyone in that building!"

He pointed and made a chopping motion with his arm, showing them the optimal line of fire to avoid hitting any of the other buildings.

The squad ran forward, zigzagging and crouching. Some dropped to the prone position and started shooting. Others fired from the kneeling position.

"Get down!" Terry yelled. Those kneeling dove into the dirt and added their firepower to the others. They fired through the windows and then systematically shot holes in the building until they assumed nothing lived. Then they conducted a bounding overwatch, some moving while others fired, then swapped until they were through the gate and set up to breach the building.

Terry recognized his training of the squad, knew they had matters well in hand. Terry motioned for third squad to take up a firing position within the compound, but only if an attack materialized from the bunkhouse where the rest of the people were.

Terry didn't want Char to go through the doorway first with him, but she insisted.

He looked into her eyes, "If you are shot, will your nanocytes heal the baby?"

She pressed her lips together and stepped back. Gene joined Terry, removed his clothes in a single motion, and became the massive Were-bear.

Terry opened the door and found the women and girls standing in a line. Three men crouched behind them.

"This is not what you want to do," Terry snarled.

"Hey, how about fuck you!" one of the men called out. Terry shifted around to see the men. They were armed with knives. "Come any closer and we start carving."

Terry turned his head and whispered where only those behind him could hear. "Get someone with a rifle to the side windows and shoot these fuckers, please."

He turned back to the line of women, seeing fear and sadness on their faces.

"Drop your knives and you live. This is your final warning."

Gene stood on his back legs and roared. He ambled forward a couple steps and the women dove for cover. The men each grabbed a hostage and held them tightly between themselves and the Were-bear.

"Hold your fire!" Terry yelled before his men started shooting.

Shonna and Char waved for the freed women and girls to go out the door. Twenty-two saved, but Terry wanted all of them.

"Joseph, would you have any insight into these three?" Terry asked, remembering that the Forsaken was with them.

"Do I ever!" he said in a sultry voice as he angled through the building, past Terry and to the side.

"Stay where you are or she dies!" one man screamed with false bravado.

"You and I both know that's not the case," Joseph said smoothly. "You're thinking how you can get out of this without dying and you're not coming up with any answers, are you? Do you see your threats intimidating my friends, or me for that matter? You don't, do you?"

The man looked away for a moment before throwing his knife behind him and clasping his hands on top of his head. The terrified woman ran straight into Char's arms and together they left the building.

"On your knees," Terry growled at the man. He got down.

"You candy ass, bailing on your buddies," a second man spit.

"Let's see what you have to think," Joseph said, maneuvering to the side away from Terry and the others.

"What the fuck are you?" he sneered through thick lips. His face was covered by a heavy black beard. The man wasn't big, but his arms were corded with muscle. He looked like one who loved to fight.

"I'm your twin brother," Joseph said, laughing. "A pariah, an outcast, whose only crime is being better than those around you, except present company, of course."

Joseph tipped his hat toward Terry and the Weres. Terry shook his head, not sure how much longer he'd let Joseph play with the bad guys.

TH hadn't done much with the .45 that he'd liberated from Cheyenne Mountain, but he felt it was time. He put his M4 on a table and removed the rest of his weapons. He took off his flak jacket and stood there in just his shirt. He loved the feel of the pistol in his hand.

"You are most likely to kill that woman, out of spite, figuring that if you're going to die, you'll take someone with you. But an innocent? There's no joy in that. How about me? Fight me and if you win, you'll have your freedom."

Terry saw how Joseph was trying to fit in with Terry's ideals. "What do you say, Colonel? A little sparring match with freedom on the line."

"There's no way he can win, Joseph. You are far better than he ever was," Terry taunted.

The man was smarter than that, although not by much. "Fuck you both. I don't trust that you won't shoot me. Give me that gun and then things will even up. I'll fight Pasty then."

Joseph tsked while shaking his head. "Nice try, needle dick." The Forsaken held his hands out to the side as he inched closer to the bearded man.

The third man was trying to get to the window, dragging the woman backwards as he moved and watched the intruders before him. The woman he was holding started to struggle.

Someone fired through the window at point blank range, exploding the third man's head and showering blood and gore over the second man, his hostage, and Joseph.

The woman started screaming, closed her eyes, and covered her ears.

"Shut up, bitch!" the last man yelled.

She didn't hear him. Terry walked the few steps to her and gripped her arm. She resisted at first but let him lead her around the Were-bear and to the door where Sue was waiting. Char had returned, grim-faced and angry.

Terry knew that look. It usually came right before someone was torn apart.

"Nice shot," Terry said toward the window.

"And then there was one," Joseph said and started clapping. "What's it feel like to be the last man standing?"

He lifted his eyebrows and looked at the man with a curious expression.

The bearded man pressed his knife harder against the woman's throat, leaving a red line on her skin. She gasped, eyes wide in terror as she thought she was going to die.

Terry slowly raised his pistol and fired into the wall over the pair's head. The man jumped back, taking the knife away from its precarious place at the woman's throat. She ducked instinctively. In a move too quick to follow, Terry dropped his aim and put a large caliber bullet through the man's forehead.

He jerked backward and flopped to the floor, his body spasming in its death throes.

Joseph leaned over the body. Terry jumped forward and grabbed the Forsaken's shoulder, unsure of what the Vampire was going to do. Char took the woman outside. Gene sat down and started licking his massive paw. For the first time in his life, people had forgotten that he was there.

Billy wasn't able to wait. He had watched Terry and the others go into the biggest building within the compound and then there was nothing. Everything looked secure to him so he strode away from the pods. Kiwi, Aaron, and Kae followed.

When Terry and Char left the building, they found

Kaeden waiting for them. Char leaned down and spoke softly. "Do you recognize any of these people, any of the girls?"

The young boy had avoided them, but Terry and Char wanted to know, so they each took a hand and walked Kaeden to the group of unkempt females who were huddling tightly together.

Terry knew that he wasn't the right person to talk with the group. He nodded to Char.

"My name is Charumati and this is my husband, Terry Henry Walton, and this little man is Kaeden. He told us a story about how men had come and taken the girls from their group of children. Are you those girls?" she asked. The oldest of the group was still young, probably in her late twenties.

The bruises on their arms and faces suggested physical abuse. The hollow expressions on their faces told a bigger story.

Akio watched from the pod, deciding that Terry needed help. Using the power of his mind, he projected calm over the women, gave them a sense of peace, if only for the moment. It would be the first step in their new lives.

Their expressions changed and the women looked at the group of warriors, the Force de Guerre, the other beautiful people, a man dressed in black leather with a wide-brimmed hat, a bear, and a dog. They didn't know what to make of the strangers, but they felt free.

At Char's urging, the women brought the young girls where Kaeden could see them, and where they could see him. They recognized Kaeden and ran to him.

Terry looked through the fence at the pod where Akio, Yuko, and Eve stood. He mouthed the words 'thank you.'

CHAPTER TWENTY-TWO

The pods couldn't carry everyone at one time, so Mark volunteered to remain behind with the platoon and scavenge the compound for anything they could get.

One man had surrendered and Terry didn't know what to do with him. He turned him over to Mark to chase away.

Akio was accommodating in leaving the well-armed platoon behind. Terry thanked Mark for his initiative. He also wanted to stay but Char suggested the delegation of authority had happened and it was the right thing to do. Mark needed the opportunity to do something in the field, out from under the watchful eye of the colonel.

Terry cautioned Mark to watch out for anyone who might return from hunting. They couldn't be certain that all the men were accounted for. The sergeant saluted and the group departed.

The pods quickly lifted off and flew to Chicago, where the two groups offloaded. Terry, Char, and her pack unloaded the ammunition and supplies, while Billy led the women to the mayor's building, where Felicity was waiting.

Akio met Terry at the back of the ramp. He bowed, deeper than before, while Terry and Char bent at the waist to exactly ninety degrees.

"I can't thank you enough, Akio-sama," Terry told him.

"It is I who should be thanking you, Master Pilot," Akio said softly. "I am sorry for the loss of your man. We will remember him."

"I can ask for nothing more. If we are true to ourselves, we cannot be false to anyone, as we learn in *Hamlet*. Thank you again, Akio-sama. Until next we meet." Terry wondered why the quote came to him, but expected Akio was in his mind and had already seen it.

Akio returned inside and closed the ramp. The empty pods departed on a return heading to pick up the platoon.

Terry, Char, Kaeden, and one of the girls, Kimber, walked together. Kae and the little girl held hands. She seemed older than him, but was a little shorter.

"I used to be taller than you," she said.

"Nah," Kaeden replied.

"You knew each other before?" Char asked innocently.

"His whole life!" Kimber replied. "He's my little brother."

Terry stopped walking. The group of women and girls stopped, too. They had no idea what was happening. They'd never traveled by air before, but did it because that's what they were told to do, believing that it would lead to freedom.

And it did. These strangers had saved them, asking for nothing in return. They wanted the happy ending. They wanted to see Kimber and Kaeden reunited. They watched, entranced by the reunion.

Terry should have been happy that Kaeden's sister had been returned. He just wished he would have known that their family was about to get bigger.

Char snickered as she saw a full range of emotions cross Terry's face. "Kimber, dear, you'll live with us as Kaeden does," she finally managed to say. The little girl looked skeptical, but her brother reassured her.

"They are the best!" Kae said of his adopted parents.

Terry started walking again. Char gasped and bent over. Terry kneeled before her. "What's wrong?" he asked.

"The little bugger has quite a kick!" She straightened up and took a deep breath. "Shall we?"

Char walked ahead as if nothing happened. In Terry's mind, his world was closing in around him. He started to breathe faster and faster until he couldn't catch his breath at all. Terry had to stop.

"TH, you're hyperventilating and probably driving your nanocytes crazy. Do you need me to punch you in the face?" Char offered.

Terry tried to hold her off with one hand, but she wouldn't move. The group of women stood and watched, finding the episode curious from a man who had so mercilessly battled their captors to win their freedom. They wondered what afflicted him, but Char seemed to think it trivial.

Char rubbed his back as he was doubled over, trying to calm himself. She smiled nervously at the other women. "My husband," she said apologetically. Some of them nodded knowingly, others were curious, and a few were still lost to the horrors within their own minds.

She took the opportunity to talk with them. "We are rebuilding civilization. Power, running water, flush toilets.

None of these things are too far away. We have a dining facility where you will eat regular meals. There is plenty of work that needs done to support the community. Farming, fishing, weaving, woodcraft. You name it and we have to do it, but we have a nice place to live here and really smart people working for the betterment of all. We are happy that you have joined us, but you are free to determine your own destiny."

Char looked from face to face. They didn't give much away with their expressions. Char knew that it would take time.

One of the women screamed. Ted was walking quickly toward them, surrounded by his wolf pack.

"They aren't dangerous, are you, my pretties?" Ted asked, looking at the shaggy grey beasts.

"Char, I just wanted to tell you that we'll be firing the plant for one hour in the morning and two hours every evening for the next few months while we bring the big power plant on line. I've set up a work schedule that should be viable. We will need more hands, though. Are any of you experienced with working in a power plant or around heavy machinery? Piping maybe?" Ted spoke quickly while looking at the women.

No one said anything as they watched the nice looking man with the pack of wolves.

"Pity," Ted said. He found Sue and for the first time in a long time, hugged her and gave her a kiss. "I'm glad you're home."

Their relationship was distant at the best of times, but it worked for them. Clyde still wasn't used to the wolves, remaining wary with his hackles up whenever they were near.

Gene, Timmons, Shonna, and Merrit grabbed Ted to get the skinny on his plan. Walking him away as he talked excitedly.

Sue watched them go without concern. It was Ted's way. Aaron stood uncomfortably behind the group, on the outside looking in as usual.

Joseph was nowhere to be seen. Char reached out with her senses and found him, walking the road alone back toward the old city of Chicago, the place he called home.

That left Terry and Char, with twenty-five women and girls. Billy was waiting inside his building, but no one could say that he was waiting patiently.

Terry finally stood up straight. The color had returned to his face. Char nuzzled his cheek and nibbled on his ear. "We'll get a house and everyone will have their own bedroom, including us, TH. Our adventure is just starting, my love. More of us sooner than we thought, but so what? As long as we are together, isn't that what matters most?"

Terry had to agree. "It is, my love."

They'd taken so long getting nowhere that the two pods returned while they were still in the open area. The pods touched down and the platoon disembarked, removing a variety of things and depositing them on the ground before returning for a second load. The ramps closed and the pods took off, having spent a total of two minutes on the ground.

Terry was immediately himself. Sergeant Mark approached, saluted, and reported that they'd found what looked like personal items. They brought it all. If the women wanted it, it would be there. If not, they would make it disappear.

"Well done, Sergeant. Across the board, today, well done. Tomorrow, no PT, breakfast and then mid-morning we'll have a ceremony for Boris, then we'll conduct an after action review for both of today's operations," Terry said crisply, then returned Mark's salute. "Carry on."

When Terry turned around, Char had her arms crossed and was tapping one foot. "You can fight a battle and order twenty-five men and women around as if it were nothing, but find out that you're going to live with three kids and you become a blubbering mess!"

Terry knew that he was supposed to be offended, but he was vastly outnumbered. "But you love me in spite of that," he tried with a shy smile. "Billy's waiting."

But he wasn't. Billy and Felicity had joined them. "Good afternoon, y'all. My name is Felicity and this is Billy Spires, the mayor of our town. Since it is dinnertime, I suggest we take this to our dining facility and get you something to eat," Felicity drawled.

Ted had led most of the others away, leaving Terry, Char, and Aaron to help carry. But once the group of women saw the load, they pitched in. With everyone carrying something, they were able to move everything to the barracks in one trip. Mark offered to house the women and girls in the spare rooms on the second floor of the FDG's barracks. With the Force on the first floor, they would be protected and hopefully they'd feel safe.

Mark was sympathetic to their plight. Not that long ago, he would not have been, but with Terry's and Char's influence, he'd starting learning more about people, about humanity.

Mark wasn't the only one who had changed. He looked around and saw the platoon, finally blooded in combat, somber yet driven.

They were professional warfighters.

CHAPTER TWENTY-THREE

The platoon stood at attention as Terry positioned himself near the rough casket in which Boris rested. They'd chosen the open field near the pharmaceutical plant as the town's cemetery. Terry was sorry to see a member of the Force as the first to be buried there. The worst part was that he wouldn't be the last.

Terry looked at the group, from one person to the next. He nodded to Kiwi and Char standing behind the formation.

He and Char would see every one of them dead and buried. They were special and didn't age like the others. In another twenty, the original members of the Force would be old, and he and Char would look the same, feel the same.

Terry knew that he would get good at delivering eulogies, the bad side of the good deal from his enhancements. The platoon shifted back and forth as the silence stretched out.

"When one of us dies, we all lose a part of ourselves. Such

is the loyalty of the FDG," Terry said while looking at the casket. He looked up at the platoon and saw them locked at the position of attention. "At ease, people."

Terry shuffled his feet as he tried to come up with something to say. He'd thought about it, but nothing had come to him, so there he was, forced to wing it. He wanted all of them to know that they deserved the very best he could give them.

"I don't want to ever get good at this, wishing people on their way and then planting them in the ground. It sucks. Boris came to us a while back, claiming to be the last of the Marines. He got his ass kicked for that, but he turned into a good one, a valued member of our family and someone who fought hard every single day."

Mark raised his hand and Terry pointed him out.

"I wanted to say a few things, if it's okay, sir," Mark said and Terry nodded, glad for the respite. "Boris and I had our differences, but that had nothing to do with the quality of warrior that he was. He earned our respect. He earned my respect. He would never ask his people to do something that he wouldn't do, and that's how he died, by leading the way."

Terry thanked Mark for his kind words and looked for anyone else to speak. Charlie raised his hand. "Me and Boris went into the interview together, saying we was the last of the Marines. I'll be goddamned if I knew that the colonel was the *real* last Marine. That wasn't too smart on our part, but we wanted to join up, be bad asses. And you know what? We learned that it wasn't about that at all. It was living to a higher ideal, making people feel safe because they knew we'd protect them. We saw that yesterday. Fuck those guys and anyone like them who comes up against us. Wherever Boris is, he knows that we won..."

Charlie stopped speaking as he sniffled and tried to gather

himself. He and Boris had been best friends. Now he was the squad leader, having taken Boris's place, and was trying to be strong for the others. He didn't look comfortable with his appointment. Terry made a mental note to talk with the man.

"For Boris, for anyone here, know that we leave no one behind. We protect those who can't protect themselves. Our job is to bring humanity back to civilization and what we saw out there yesterday…two shining examples of how people used their power for the wrong reasons. Well, the Force de Guerre is here to stay. Those people can go *fuck* themselves!" Terry yelled, angry but proud.

"Boris died to give humanity a chance to be human," Terry continued. "Any one of us could be in that box, so we will train harder, we will work harder to be that much better than our enemies, because the people we protect deserve our best. Akio said he may have a few more jobs that need doing, and there is no one better to do them than *us*. Take the rest of the day off, go fishing, go for a walk, play a game, do something where you revel in life. Tomorrow, we start training again. Sergeant, take charge of the platoon and carry out the plan of the day."

Mark brought the platoon to attention and saluted.

Charlie led a detail to drop the casket into the hole and then fill it. They didn't have a headstone, only a wooden plank. Mark said he'd take care of that since the Force deserved better.

Terry agreed.

Terry shook hands with everyone there. These were his people. He'd made them what they were, and then he put them in harm's way.

And he'd do it again, because that was why the Force de Guerre existed.

Akio had hinted that there was more work to do, a lot more. Terry already had a plan in mind, where they'd train and that they'd help in the power plant, or the fields, or with fishing. Full days stretched out before them like an endless plain.

A busy Marine is a happy Marine, Terry thought. *Or, a bored Marine is a liberty risk, taking their time off and wreaking havoc on the local town.*

He didn't know why he thought that, but he was always worried when his people weren't training or in combat.

Char waited for him to finish before approaching him and taking his hand. He spoke first. "They're not Marines, but they are."

She didn't know what he wanted from her, so she talked about what she wanted to talk about. "Nice ceremony. No wailing or gnashing of teeth, just the loyalty and dedication you give them and demand back. They're proud of what they've done, TH. You made that happen. Yesterday was a great day. It validated the FDG as a global force for good." She paused a moment, a smile playing on her lips, "As hokey as that sounds."

"It did, didn't it?" Terry forced a smile. "Bringing humanity back to civilization has its challenges, doesn't it?"

"It started with Sawyer Brown. He needed to go. Once he was gone, look what happened? The people flourished," Char said, looking intensely at Terry. Her purple eyes sparkled as the morning sun shone on her face. The silver in her hair glittered. "No, TH, this is exactly where you need to be and doing what you need to do. People are going to die. Where in the hell did they get armor-piercing ammunition, and how were we supposed to plan for that?"

Terry drank in her beauty and wisdom.

"I think we'll call them warriors, not Marines, not soldiers, but warriors. Who else would serve in the Force of War?"

"Do you *even* hear anything I'm saying to you, Terry Henry Walton?" Char said, smiling. She knew her husband. She knew he heard it all. And she knew that he knew that she was right. "You are such a man."

❖ ❖ ❖

Autumn Dawn was sick again. Her age and the journey had taken its toll. She seemed to always be cold. Rapids and Winter Rain were worried. Kiwi started spending more time with her grandmother. Geronimo was there too, not missing training but being relieved of the work details during the time that his family needed him.

Which meant that he was there for his wife. Terry had seen those who weren't there for their spouses in times of need. He saw a lot of divorces and too many broken men.

He wouldn't let that happen. Gerry said that he could work every other day and the colonel flatly refused as he played the age and wisdom card, saying, "You may not think this is the best use of your time right now, but trust me in that later, you'll know that it was the best thing you could have done. Your marriage will be stronger, and you will be a better man for it."

Sometimes Terry had to lecture. He'd hate to waste all the lessons he'd learned the hard way.

When Terry, Char, Kaeden, and Kimber stopped by, Autumn Dawn was sitting up, bundled into a cocoon of blankets, one of which was a buffalo hide. Terry could only smile. He and Char had killed the buffalo, but lost their blankets with the fire they'd started. They had to trade the hide for new blankets, which they continued to use to this day.

"You look great," Terry said with a smile, offering Charumati the chair next to the old woman.

"You lie poorly," the old woman croaked. Terry wanted to laugh, but the whole situation reminded him of Black Feather. Terry and Char had been there when he took his last breath.

Autumn Dawn knew what he was thinking and said reassuringly, "I'm not ready to go just yet."

"We only wanted to stop by and see how you were doing," Char said softly. "Is there anything you need from us?"

"Only your continued support and encouragement of my granddaughter. She is a fine young woman," the old woman said slowly. Gerry stood against a wall, hugging Kiwi from behind as she rested her hands on his.

"I'm sorry, but we also wanted to introduce Kaeden's sister, Kimber," Terry offered, thrusting the little girl forward. She started to struggle and Autumn Dawn laughed.

"That tells me how I really look," she managed to say through heavy breaths, trying to smile and lifting a shriveled hand to pat the girl's head. "Welcome to our family, little one."

The old lady's eyes closed and she seemed to drift off to sleep. Terry and Char excused themselves and it took no urging for the kids to run outside.

Terry stopped and looked at Gerry and Kiwi. "Hold on to what you have with everything you've got," he told them as he gently rested a hand on Gerry's shoulder. With a quick nod, Terry left.

◈ ◈ ◈

"We need more food, Billy," Sue said without looking at any of the papers in front of her.

"Tell me something I don't know?" Billy snapped back.

"You love Clyde," Sue replied without hesitation. The dog had been lying beneath the table and stood when he heard his name, expecting a treat or to go outside.

He was good with either.

"That dog! He'd let me starve. Honestly, how much can one dog eat?"

Sue shrugged, unsure that Clyde had ever reached his limit.

"We have too many people and not enough good ideas," Billy conceded.

"You know what that means, Billy dear," Felicity said from her seat on the couch. Marcie was fast asleep next to her.

"I don't," Billy replied, turning to look at her. She'd been losing weight, as had he. The rigors of the office, too much work to do with too little was taking its toll on both of them.

Felicity looked at him and chuckled. "Why, Billy dear, you need to ask for help." It seemed simple to her, but not to a man like Billy Spires.

His eyebrows flicked up at the revelation. He turned to Sue. "Please gather the people who I need to ask for help, so I can ask them for help."

"What do you think they're going to tell you?" Sue asked.

"That we need to fish more, that we need to go on a major hunt, harvest buffalo or whatever else is big and huntable. Send a foraging group out to find wild vegetables. Maybe use the vehicles to transport these groups beyond our normal reach," the mayor stated succinctly.

"There's the Billy I fell in love with!" Felicity exclaimed.

"So what do you need me to do?" Sue asked.

"Get the people who need to be in charge of each of those things so I can tell them what we need from them and they can tell me how they're going to accomplish those things. I'll need Terry and Char, and then Blevin, too, from the motor pool," Billy said with a small shake of his head.

He was amazed at how simple it was once all the distractions were removed, the noise silenced. The way ahead was revealed.

"Thanks, you two," Billy said, looking from one to the other. "For everything."

❖ ❖ ❖

Maria and Pepe drove the dune buggy. They would have preferred their cart, but it was with the group driving the cattle.

They'd been busy working the soil, preparing for the spring planting and once they got their first seeds into the ground in their ad hoc greenhouse, they were tasked with going north and finding the other farmers who seemed to be little more than ghosts.

They wouldn't ride the horses, but when Terry offered the dune buggy, Pepe perked up. Maria wasn't so sure, but after a few practice drives, Terry turned them loose. Coordinating with farms that were already producing was critical for immediate viability. They didn't have years to wait in order to produce something in the quantities they needed.

James squeezed into the dune buggy on their first couple trips, having to stand between the seats as if manning the machinegun. He guided them to the corner where he and Lacy had left various gifts for the farmers. They stopped the dune buggy there and James pointed out where he thought the farmers were hiding.

Pepe and Maria looked at the field as if they were kids seeing a playground. Without waiting for permission, they got out of the vehicle and worked their way through a broken fence, heading into the cultivated soil. Pepe took a handful of the rich black dirt and sniffed it. He held it out to Maria but she politely declined.

James stayed with the dune buggy while the two farmers continued into the field, just like James and Lacy had done how many times before. When they reached a small building, someone stepped out and blocked their way.

"Hi, I'm Pepe and this is Maria. My compliments to you on the quality of your soil. This really is magnificent. What do you grow?" Pepe asked innocently, disregarding the way the man held his shovel as if it was a weapon.

The man didn't answer.

"We brought seed packs from our place out in Colorado. The weather got too hot, so here we are. I think our tomatoes would grow magnificently, be bursting full in this soil and with the longer growing season. I didn't catch your answer, what do you grow?" Pepe pressed. Maria stood by patiently and watched.

"We grow beans and peppers. Lost our tomato seeds a few years back. You got tomato seeds?" the man asked.

Pepe stuck out his hand. "Yes, we do, and we'd love to share and trade…"

CHAPTER TWENTY-FOUR

The next two months were a blur, until Chief Foxtail's scouts rode up to the power plant. Terry had the platoon spread out grinding and banging away refurbishing piping as Timmons directed.

They'd had to dismantle a quarter of the old plant in order to build a stock of supplies to work on the system that Timmons was trying to bring back to life.

The riders waved when they saw Terry. He thrust a fist in the air and yelled a mighty oorah. The others working nearby joined him to greet the new arrivals.

"They are not far behind us, Terry Henry Walton," the first scout reported.

"I can't tell you how great it is to see you and hear the news. We can bring some trucks out if people are tired of walking?" Terry offered. The two on horseback conferred for a moment.

"That would be greatly appreciated. The people are tired, for the journey has been long," the man said in a tired voice.

"Rally up!" Terry bellowed, then issued orders to his men, who took off running toward the base where First Sergeant Blevin's motor pool was located.

Ten minutes later, the buses and three trucks rolled up. The scouts waved at them to follow and rode away.

Terry yelled at the drivers to take the people to the base. The first sergeant gave the thumbs up and led the small convoy away.

"Corporal Lacy!" the colonel called as he entered the plant. She yelled back and waved from three catwalks up. "The rest of our people and the cattle are here! You keep things running and then wrap up early. I'm sure we'll have a big party tonight. Be there or be square!"

Lacy didn't get the odd phrase, but she understood what she needed to do—be in charge and wrap early. She could do that. Corporal Lacy saluted quickly and then ran off to let the warriors know.

Terry headed for the base, running fast like only an enhanced human could. He covered the mile in less than three minutes.

Not bad for a senior citizen, he thought. He hadn't even broken a sweat. He slowed as he ran through the base so he wouldn't alarm the civilians. If someone had seen him running, they could think there was an emergency.

He ran straight into Billy's office. "They're here, Billy, our people, Chief Foxtail, his people, and the cattle. They made it, Billy!"

The mayor smiled broadly, leaning back in his chair and putting his hands behind his head.

"Why do you sound surprised, TH?" Billy asked.

"I was going for pleasantly surprised and delighted with a dash of oorah on top," Terry countered.

"I'd say you accomplished some of that," Sue offered.

"Come on, Clyde. Let's greet some new people," Terry said, bending down. Clyde's nails slid on the marble as he ran from under the table and headed for the door. Billy, Felicity, and Marcie packed up to walk out as well. Sue decided there was no sense in staying.

When they got outside, Kaeden and Kimber were running across the open area, yelling something unintelligible. Terry bolted for them, sliding to a stop and taking a knee.

"Come on, Dad. Mom says it's time," Kae said, grabbing Terry's hand and trying to pull him.

"It's time!" he yelled, looking back at Sue. "Take Clyde. I have to go."

He picked up both kids and ran for his home. Char was there alone and the baby was coming.

❖ ❖ ❖

The scouts led the vehicles to the conglomeration of people walking with the herd of cattle. Blevin popped the door open and offered a ride to anyone who was tired of walking. The buses and trucks filled quickly, leaving only those riding horses or driving carts.

The scouts told the Weathers boys and Eli's family to catch the bus. The riders would use the horses to bring the cattle the rest of the way.

It took no time to cover the five miles back to the base.

The small convoy pulled through the main gate and maneuvered to drop the newcomers off at the main building, where Billy and Felicity greeted them. Sue had taken Clyde, but then she and the dog followed Terry to be with Char.

Chief Foxtail was first off the bus, taking a moment to thank Blevin for coming for them.

"Mayor Billy Spires, I am so happy to see you and this wonderful place," the chief said in way of greeting.

"We have food, we have shelter, and soon, we'll have power, too. For your people, we have plenty of work that needs to be done. Farming, ranching, fishing, exploring, ironwork. There's so much to do, but I could talk about that until the cows come home." Billy chuckled at his own joke, then he shook himself.

"You need to go see Autumn Dawn. She's been sick lately." Billy didn't elaborate. He waved at the chief to follow him as he walked away, leaving Felicity to greet the new arrivals and get them going in the direction of the quarters they'd be getting.

Billy and the chief walked quickly to see Autumn Dawn, who was barely able to lift her eyelids. Foxtail crouched next to her. "Mother, I've made it home," he told her.

Her eyelids fluttered, but she didn't open her eyes. Her lips worked and finally she was able to whisper, "I waited for this. One comes and one goes."

She relaxed into her recliner-turned-bed and with a smile on her old face, she passed into Mother Earth's arms.

Gerry and Kiwi ran up, out of breath. Kiwi hung her head. "I saw Metaguas and knew it was time, Father," Kiwi said as she sought comfort in his arms. Geronimo stood close by, waiting patiently. Foxtail gave him a questioning look.

Gerry pointed to Kiwi and then grasped one of his own wrists in each hand in the sign of a partnership. Foxtail understood, smiling easily as he held his daughter.

A throat-rending scream came from far off. With a nod, the chief sent Gerry running. He followed the sound and slowed when he realized it was coming from the colonel's quarters.

◈ ◈ ◈

Char had the death grip on Terry's arm as Sue tried to talk Char through it. The contractions were gut-wrenching, forcing Char to flex as if every muscle in her body cramped at the same time. She unloaded with a scream of pain as each new wave flowed through her.

She dug her nails into Terry's arm, drawing blood. He grinned and bore it. "You did this to me!" she growled in a surreal voice.

"It'll be over soon, honey, and our little girl will be with us!" Terry tried to console her. Char's purple eyes were on fire, her face contorted.

"I'll fucking rip your fucking face off, you fuck!" Char hissed.

Terry maintained a usual sense of fear of his wife, but at that moment, it was beyond that.

He was very afraid.

Char let out another ear-piercing scream that would have shattered glass had there been any.

"I see the head," Sue said excitedly. It was everyone's first except for Margie Rose, who stood nearby with her hands over her ears. She gave Sue direction, but was afraid of getting punched or kicked or gouged. She was appalled at Char's language, admitting that she'd never seen anyone turn into one of hell's demons before.

Char gritted her teeth and grabbed Terry's arm in both

her hands. He grunted in pain, but knew he had best not say anything.

With one final push, the baby was born. The little girl belted out a piercing cry, reminiscent of her mother from only moments before, then the baby huffed and shivered. Sue swaddled her in an old shirt. It was all they had.

"Care to cut the umbilical cord?" Sue asked. Terry whipped out his knife, but Char grabbed his arm and glared at the silvered blade.

"Oh crap." He jumped up, saw Gerry outside, and demanded the man's knife. Gerry handed it over without question. Terry did the deed and Sue tied the end closed with a small piece of string.

Terry wiped the blade and handed it back.

"Autumn Dawn has passed away," Gerry said quietly. "I need to go."

Terry watched Geronimo walk quickly away. Kiwi intercepted him and they talked briefly before returning. Chief Foxtail was coming.

Inside, Char was exhausted but exhilarated. Terry rubbed his arms as he returned to Char's side. She smiled at him. "I love you," she said, smiling radiantly, purple eyes glowing. Seeing the look on his face, she was confused. "What?"

"I love you, too?" he tried.

"Did I say something? I'd heard that at times like this the inner evil Werewolf comes out. I don't remember any of it, thank goodness."

"Neither do I, lover," Terry snickered, shaking his head, but then he turned serious. "Autumn Dawn has passed away, and Foxtail is here."

"I thought she might. It was her time, and she was more than ready. They made it! That is good news." She continued to smile and rocked gently as she held her daughter.

"Name?" Terry asked, thinking he knew what the final decision had been.

"Cordelia Dawn. Cordelia from *King Lear* and Dawn for a new dawn ushered in when one passes away and for the one we have to live without. The sun still rises," Char said.

The lights flickered as the power plant came online. Chief Foxtail couldn't take his eyes from the electric bulb as it hummed and brightened.

"It has been so long," he started, then turned to Terry and Char. "Congratulations."

The baby fussed and Char finally was able to look at her baby girl. A full head of black hair with a silver streak on the side. Her little ears were fuzzy and a touch pointed. Terry studied her closely. She looked like a normal baby except for the silver streak and fuzzy ears.

"Is she a Werewolf?" Terry asked.

"Does it matter?" Char replied.

THE END

OF

NOMAD'S FURY

Terry Henry Walton will return in Nomad's Justice,
May 2017

Don't stop now! Keep turning the pages as both Craig & Michael talk about their thoughts on this book and the overall project called the Terry Henry Walton Chronicles. And artwork! There's a picture of something hiding back there that you must see.

AUTHOR'S NOTES - CRAIG MARTELLE

Written: February 28, 2017

Michael suggested that we bring all the collaborating authors to Fox, Alaska where the distractions are at a minimum. We've gotten a massive amount of snowfall and on top of that, we've had some mind numbing cold spells.

The snow is nearly up to our windows and we had temperatures to minus 50 Fahrenheit. We found out that my wife's Jeep Wrangler's thermometer topped out at -37F when the actual outside temp was -45F. I wonder if Jeep contemplated that their vehicles would be stalwart at those temps and that the drivers would be a little bummed that the display was showing it to be much warmer than it really was.

Regardless, I love writing and I love the feedback I get, whether in comments on my blog, comments on my Facebook posts, direct messages, emails, and most importantly in the reviews you leave for me on Amazon and on Goodreads.

Here is my new favorite review from Ralph Foster – you are the best!

"This is one of the greatest series I have ever read! A lot of series seem to have characters brake character just to further the plot or to fill plot holes. Not this series every character feels like a real and unique person no characters that are just plot devices. Best of all the story is believable and really allows you to get immersed in the story. Basically no wtf did they do that for moments or scratching your head at motivations of certain characters. All in all a great post apocalyptic/ romance/action series that I would recommended to anyone!"

Some other highlights from reviews that are both humbling and motivating. We come back time after time to our keyboards and work hard to deliver the best stories we can. Thank you to the reviewers who posted these great tidbits. We respect your desire for anonymity.

"I think it's a very good story without a lot of gratuitous sex. Shows a task of honor that is missing in most modern novels."

"This series can stand alone due to the great characters and well-written pacing and world-development. You don't NEED the back-story of those other "lines" in the Universe to enjoy this series."

"I will have to admit that this is turning out to be one of my favorite Kurtherian sub-series. Post-apocalyptic, pioneering, xxx kicking fun. And a quality story coming out fast and furious."

"A grand stand hit for Craig, the story cannot be put down and the ride gets better."

On a side note, how do we pronounce the names? The sanskrit spelling is Charumati, but the pronunciation is SHarumati. SH is a little further back in the throat kind of in between CH and SH, but it's easier to say and flows more smoothly by using the SH pronunciation.

A shout out to my fellow Marine Justin Sloan as we coordinated the buildup of events to make sure that the next six books in the Terry Henry Walton Chronicles flow smoothly into his books as well as into Michael's Dark Messiah. Justin was easy to work with and quick to reply to save me from writing something that wouldn't jive.

A personal thank you to Kat Lind who helped see some things I was doing that lessened the impact of the characters and the emotions within the scenes. She also helped with the developmental editing to ensure that the stories are hitting on all cylinders. Diane Velasquez and Dorene Johnson continue to take great care of me on a developmental edit side. Same thing to my fabulous editor Mia Darien, who keeps all of my books on track, seeing things that need to be seen and giving me a high level of consistency across all my titles.

And finally, the winner of the naming contest is Angie Simon who offered Cordelia from King Lear because of her love and loyalty. I'll gift you the next couple books in this series as a way to say thank you for helping me out.

The naming contest also helped me fill a gap with little Kaeden's sister. Both Beck Young and Jefferey Turk Sr who offered Kember/Kimber. The K theme resonated so that's what we went with. And then there were five. Terry Henry Walton, hard ass, tough guy, family man.

❖ ❖ ❖

If you liked this story, you might like some of my other books. You can join my mailing list by dropping by my website www.craigmartelle.com or if you have any comments, shoot me a note at craig@craigmartelle.com. I am always happy to hear from people who've read my work. I try to answer every email I receive.

If you liked the story, please write a short review for me on Amazon. I greatly appreciate any kind words, even one or two sentences go a long way. The number of reviews an ebook receives greatly improves how well an ebook does on Amazon.

Amazon – www.amazon.com/author/craigmartelle
Facebook – www.facebook.com/authorcraigmartelle
My web page – www.craigmartelle.com
Twitter – www.twitter.com/rick_banik

Thank you for reading Terry Henry Walton Chronicles!

AUTHOR'S NOTES - MICHAEL ANDERLE

Written: March 14, 2017

THANK YOU for not only reading this story, but stopping by the Author Notes to check it out!

Amazing changes in such a little amount of time.

This book is coming out in the same month as the last one, in fact, less than 11 days since the last one.

Freaking Awesome Craig is going to OWN March. He's a beast when it comes to writing. When I grow up, I think I might want to be him.

Then again, he lives in Alaska…The home of freeze-your-damned-fingers-off if you go outside, so you have to work inside. Screw that, I'll stay in Texas for now.

We are days away from releasing a new genre book "Restricted: The Rise of Magic - Hannah's Tale."

As soon as we have a freaking cover….Grumble grumble fizzle snort.

We are working in 3d modeling to help some cover art in the future…That is only going so-so. Seem's getting 3d to work is NOT easy for rigging and bone structure and clothes and clipping and stuff. I hope that we have some success in the next week or two - time will tell.

There is a LOT going on, so I'm going to make this real short and encourage you read the "Confessions" notes right after this and keep the fun up!

Best Regards,
Michael

CONFESSIONS OF A NO-COVER-TALENT AUTHOR

Every book has a cover. Everywhere you look, there's a book cover. How hard can it be? Really, how hard can it be?

This was my first book, and I did the cover myself! I know, it's hard to tell, isn't it?

HOLY FUCK! If you didn't wince and gasp in agony, then you are just like me, a no-cover-talent sumbitch.

Or, you are really, really kind to no-cover-talent people such as myself - bless you.

How do you find a good cover artist if you don't know anything or anyone in the business? That was my real challenge. Google failed me in my numerous searches using keywords like "Make my story look great with your awesome cover."

I published *It's Not Enough* with the cover you see here. I know this may sound surprising, but I didn't sell a whole lot of copies of that book.

The demographic that clicked most on the ad? Girls aged 13-17 because it appeared to be a self-help kind of book. Not one sale to that demographic, for reference. If you are into teen girl non-fiction, I recommend you use that title.

For post-apocalyptic survival fiction, not so much…

But the book was out there. I then found a relatively inexpensive pre-made cover artist and paid hundreds of dollars for three covers. The unfortunate thing is that they didn't hit the genre of my books. Those were the first books in my Free Trader series.

Do you like cats? That series has cats, snarky cats that are helping their humans rebuild civilization after a devastating civil world. It happens to be on a planet about 4000 light years away. Science fiction adventure in the style of Gregor and the Underworld (Suzanne Collins' – Hunger Games – other series) and Anne McCaffrey's Dragonriders of Pern series.

The covers didn't do any of that, but by being published, it helped me find people who could help, real artists. I was talking with Michael Anderle about something completely different, and he suggested in one minute about thirteen times that I should change my covers. We weren't talking about my books or publishing, but he snuck it in there anyway.

I found Tom Edwards, and since I had books out, he came on board with the covers for the first three, then the next three, and is contracted to do the three after that. I should have the covers for Free Trader 7-9 by mid-May.

THE FREE TRADER SERIES

Free on Kindle Unlimited. Exclusive to Amazon

I love Tom Edwards' work, and these covers helped people to pick the book up and give it a try. Hundreds of four and five-star reviews tell me that people like the story. I think it's good for all ages, and the readers agree.

FYI - the Free Trader series page on Amazon US is here. https://www.amazon.com/gp/product/ B01G19OHTS

Remember that first book? By having it published, I was able to get it in front of a small-press outfit. They liked the story a lot, but the first conversation about the book included the words, "We have to change the title, and we have to change the covers."

I didn't know anything about selling books, but I did know that in its current form, the book was dead. They also said that the story needed to be both shorter and longer. We'd accomplish that by breaking the first story in two, adding some text, and then delivering a third book, which thanks to an overwhelming response, became a fourth book, too.

And thanks to Monique Lewis Happy, Winlock Press, and Christian Bentulan, this is what that first book became – a four book series with titles and covers that gave the reader a better look at what they'd find inside.

Reader feedback was overwhelmingly positive and that matters to me.

The End Times Alaska series page on Amazon US. https://www.amazon.com/End-Times-Alaska-4-Book/dp/B01N6PVZ1V

I write because I like telling stories, but if the readers don't like the characters or the stories, then I'm not doing what I'm trying to do. Thousands of readers have told me that they love the stories. I can't ask for better than that.

As a new author, it's really important to build your readership in one genre. I didn't do that. I dicked that up twelve different ways from Sunday. I wrote a thriller, a pseudo-autobiography that is arguably, the best thing I've ever written. *People Raged and the Sky Was on Fire*, the first in the Rick Banik Thriller series (there is only one, but there will be a Rick Banik short story in an anthology to be released this summer - 2017).

That cover leaves things open. I like it and the book, but I've only sold some 50 copies total. I have the audiobook of it as well, narrated by the uber-talented fellow Alaskan, Basil Sands.

https://www.amazon.com/dp/B01GCWLGW0

I love my space opera! That's what I read for fun.

I am writing a spin-off series from the Free Trader that takes place in space. It is the Cygnus Space Opera. I asked Christian Bentulan who is a pure artist if he did space covers. He said no. I persisted, he said he'd try, and I wanted a unique spaceship. I didn't want anything from stock art. So Christian came through with the following covers for me. Pretty freaking sweet!

Cygnus Space Opera series page on Amazon US.
https://www.amazon.com/dp/B01NCYLI1A

Holy crap what a journey! It took me six months to get in front of the cover artists once they were on board. It also helped to get that bestseller tag on books to share with the artists. They are happy to get their work seen and appreciated by tens of thousands of people.

And then there's the work with Michael Anderle. These covers were done by Andrew Dobell out of the UK and this is the second set. The first were done using Photoshop using stock images. We needed that to make sure the series was going to resonate with the readership. It did, overwhelmingly so, so we decided to hire models and do a real photo shoot from which to build a consistent brand for the covers.

The Terry Henry Walton Chronicles counts on a certain frequency of release. Our readers go through these fairly quickly. Nomad Supreme had to wait on eBay UK and some other commercial providers to deliver the props that we purchased as well as the time it took Andrew to find the models and gather everything in one place at one time. It took longer than I wanted, but I am somewhat separated from the real world living in the sub-Arctic.

When everything finally came to fruition, you see that the models and all-original covers were worth the wait. Patience is a bitter cup from which only the strong may drink. I keep telling myself that, although every time Andrew asks when I want something, I always tell him "yesterday."

The Terry Henry Walton Chronicles series page on Amazon US.
https://www.amazon.com/gp/product/B01NAW-TOH3

Each was painful in its own right because I don't know dick about artsy shit.

I can't stop being me, but I learned most importantly that I should not have anything to do with covers, besides describing the genre, general topic, and let the artist do what artists do.

Those final covers are for short stories or anthologies that I've done. I put together the first three to help both new and established authors increase visibility and acquire another revenue stream. It's hard being an author as you are it. If you don't write or market, then you don't get paid.

In any case, there's my story of how a complete cover moron has such great covers on his books. I got help, lots and lots of help.

Peace, fellow humans.

Amazon – www.amazon.com/author/craigmartelle
Facebook – www.facebook.com/authorcraigmartelle
My web page – www.craigmartelle.com
Twitter – www.twitter.com/rick_banik

Thank you for reading this story.

THE TERRY HENRY WALTON CHRONICLES

THE KUTHERIAN GAMBIT SERIES

Book 1 – Nomad Found
Book 2 – Nomad Redeemed
Book 3 - Nomad Unleashed
Book 4 - Nomad Supreme
Book 5 – Nomad's Fury
Book 6 – Nomad Justice
Book 7 – Nomad Avenged
Book 8 – Nomad Mortis
Book 9 – Nomad's Force
Book 10 – Nomad's Galaxy

FREE TRADER SERIES

Book 1 – The Free Trader of Warren Deep
Book 2 – The Free Trader of Planet Vii
Book 3 – Adventures on RV Traveler
Book 4 – Battle for the Amazon
Book 5 – Free the North!
Book 6 – Free Trader on the High Seas
Book 7 – Southern Discontent (2017)
Book 8 – The Great 'Cat Rebellion (2017)
Book 9 – Return to the Traveler (2017)

CYGNUS SPACE OPERA - SET IN THE FREE TRADER UNIVERSE

Book 1 – Cygnus Rising
Book 2 – Cygnus Expanding
Book 3 – Cygnus Arrives (2017)

END TIMES ALASKA SERIES, A WINLOCK PRESS PUBLICATION

Book 1: Endure
Book 2: Run
Book 3: Return
Book 4: Fury

RICK BANIK THRILLERS

People Raged and the Sky Was on Fire
The Heart Raged (2017)
Paranoid in Paradise (Short Story - 2017)

SHORT STORY CONTRIBUTIONS TO ANTHOLOGIES

Earth Prime Anthology, Volume 1
(Stephen Lee & James M. Ward)
Apocalyptic Space Short Story Collection
(Stephen Lee & James M. Ward)
Lunar Resorts Anthology, Volume 2
(Stephen Lee & James M. Ward)
Just One More Fight
(published as a novella standalone)
The Expanding Universe, Volume 1
(edited by Craig Martelle)
The Expanding Universe, Volume 2
(edited by Craig Martelle – June 2017)
The Misadventures of Jacob Wild McKilljoy
(with Michael-Scott Earle)
Metamorphosis Alpha, Stories from the Starship
Warden
(with James M. Ward – Summer 2017)

MICHAEL ANDERLE

KUTHERIAN GAMBIT SERIES TITLES INCLUDE:

RECLAIMING HONOR
With Justin Sloan

Justice Is Calling (01)
Claimed By Honor (02)
Judgment Is Coming (03)
Angel of Reckoning (04) (*Soon*)

THE ETHERIC ACADEMY
With TS Paul

ALPHA CLASS (01)
ALPHA CLASS (02)
ALPHA CLASS (03) (*Early Summer 2017*)

TERRY HENRY "TH" WALTON CHRONICLES
With Craig Martelle

Book 1 – Nomad Found
Book 2 – Nomad Redeemed
Book 3 - Nomad Unleashed
Book 4 - Nomad Supreme
Book 5 – Nomad's Fury
Book 6 – Nomad Justice
Book 7 – Nomad Avenged
Book 8 – Nomad Mortis
Book 9 – Nomad's Force
Book 10 – Nomad's Galaxy

SHORT STORIES
Frank Kurns Stories of the Unknownworld 01 (*7.5*)
You Don't Mess with John's Cousin
Frank Kurns Stories of the Unknownworld 02 (*9.5*)
Bitch's Night Out
Frank Kurns Stories of the Unknownworld 03 (13.25)
BELLATRIX
With Natalie Grey

AUDIOBOOKS
Available at Audible.com and iTunes

THE KURTHERIAN GAMBIT
Death Becomes Her - Available Now
Queen Bitch – Available Now
Love Lost – Coming Soon

RECLAIMING HONOR SERIES
Justice Is Calling – Available Now
Claimed By Honor – Available Now

TERRY HENRY "TH" WALTON CHRONICLES
Nomad Found
Nomad Redeemed – Coming Soon

THE ETHERIC ACADEMY
Alpha Class
Alpha Class 2 – Coming Soon

ANTHOLOGIES
Glimpse
Honor in Death
(Michael's First Few Days)

Beyond the Stars: At Galaxy's Edge
Tabitha's Vacation

CRAIG MARTELLE SOCIAL

For a chance to see ALL of Craig's new Book Series
Check out his website below!

Website:
http://www.craigmartelle.com

Email List:
http://www.craigmartelle.com
(Go 1/2 way down his first page, the box is in the center!)

Facebook Here:
https://www.facebook.com/AuthorCraigMartelle/

MICHAEL ANDERLE SOCIAL

Website:
http://kurtherianbooks.com/

Email List:
http://kurtherianbooks.com/email-list/

Facebook Here:
https://www.facebook.com/TheKurtherianGambitBooks/

Made in the USA
San Bernardino, CA
13 September 2019